Devadasi

Maya Goray

Vitasta

Published by
Renu Kaul Verma
Vitasta Publishing Pvt Ltd
2/15, Ansari Road, Daryaganj
New Delhi - 110 002
info@vitastapublishing.com

ISBN: 978-93-86473-98-1

First Edition 2021
MRP ₹ 399

Typeset & Cover Design by Somesh Kumar Mishra
Printed by Vikas Computer and Printers

For my dearest daughter

Prologue

It is a photograph typical of the Raj. Against the hazy sepia background of the bungalow, the foreground figures of the Smythes come into focus; on the lawn a young English boy sits on a pony, his proud parents stand on either side, holding its bridle. Their infant girl is carried on her ayah's hip, the servant an inadvertent and unwelcome inclusion in the family portrait.

But I'm getting ahead of myself.

I am the storyteller, Sutradhara, narrator in traditional Indian plays, whose role extended to stage manager and impresario. Sutra means string thread, or yarn – which is what I intend spinning you [the first of my puns – playing with words is part of my job]. Sutradhara, 'thread holder'. My job description probably comes from the fact that he once used puppets to tell his story, a string-puller, though *I* will not be *manipulating* my characters.

Another pun! Didn't you get that? Well, from now I'll ping* to alert you to my puns.

Wait, I'm not done with the word: sutra is also to sew or stitch, yes the same root as suture, and therefore "a thread that runs through and holds things together". Sutras were aphoristic rules etched on palm leaves, held together with string.

My job often resembled a combination of rag picker and tailor: I collected scraps of information and sewed them into a crazy-quilt of a story, a security blanket that also caught my dreams. I'd snip and tack on improvisations; I'd add odds and ends needed to jog my memory so that my patchwork served to keep me on the narrative path, the backdrop against which my characters played out their parts. As Shakespeare said … but why should I quote him, he too often has the last word in most matters. My collage also served as a picture book for illiterate villagers – not that you westernised intellectuals need any such visual aid.

I have been supplanted by television – the flying carpet has landed as the magic box – so that those yokels no longer gather under the largest peepul tree to hear my stories. But here's an irony: I find myself in demand once more because "Storytelling" has come full circle, being researched, recorded, analysed … and my breed now goes on tour, narrating stories to urbanites like you.

I believe you lot are mostly "foreign-returned"? What a mixed bunch: sociologist, anthropologist, feminist, a researcher into story-telling, a psychologist examining ways of relating in Hindu myths – and hah, techies!

> [Rishab: I am, but maybe not all the others?
> Akhil: No, I'm not a techie, but yes, I think we're all probably i-Gen'ers.
> SD: i-Genners? What's that?
> Rishab: You can't be a wordsmith, dude, unless you update your vocab! i-Gen: internet-generation, Gen Z, those who have never lived without the internet.]

Well, we'll see how your virtual worlds compare with my maya of multiple realities, those I created for my old audiences. I overstep the lakshman rekha of time-space; I'm able to see past, present and future simultaneously from my vantage point. The satellite is your eye in the sky but I am clairvoyant and clairaudient as well; god-like, though I don't descend* to the mechanics of melodramatic reversals of fortune or to contrived endings.

My traditional listeners didn't question this stance, they took these abilities for granted. And you, my post-millennial audience, should have no problem with it; you are as gullible – in your i-Gen way! You readily accept your virtual reality, and those techi-toys give you similar powers: you range through cyberspace, see faces that are thousands of miles away, hear multiple voices, you can morph people or objects … the same fairytale ingredients that we storytellers have been using for centuries!

All is permitted the storyteller and I have the best

antecedent: my prototype, Vyasa, was not only narrator of a wondrous tale but also an actor in it. And, if you will not allow me these indulgences of omniscience and omnipresence, why then, the fabric that I am so carefully fashioning, will simply fall apart: no story, no leela, no maya, illusion.

Rending the veil of maya results in revelation.

> [Sagarika: But that's exactly what apocalypse is!
> Advik: What's doomsday got to do with … ?
> Sagarika: Absolutely nothing! No, the Greek word apokálypsis means "lifting the veil", "revelation": when something unknown can only be known when unveiled!
> Christians came up with that end-of-the-world crap, as they gradually equated the word with Armageddon.]

Makes you wonder who borrowed from whom, doesn't it? As I was saying, it is only for mortals who have already reached great heights of spirituality and are knocking on sahasrar, like someone trying to push the attic trapdoor open. Lesser mortals are content with rupturing the veil at the crass level, the hymen. My story veers more towards this grosser plane.

[What's sahasrar? Looks like you've been out of India too long, Akhil]. The cranial region is an oubliette and sahasrar is its trapdoor to the Infinite. Sahasrar is the apex chakra, goal of the kundalini serpent that rises from the lowest chakra in the urogenital region. It is the apple of supreme knowledge, forbidden to Adam and Eve, till the serpent puts it within (wo)man's reach: instant nirvana when sahasrar, the thousand-petalled lotus opens, bursting through the top of the head!

Which reminds me: that bump on Buddha's head was not sartorial. They say it was actually his sahasrar that broke through when he attained moksha, but he postponed his nirvana: he was not ready to leave the world, he still had much to accomplish, to make mortals understand his message. So he covered the half-emerged sahasrar with his hair. His top-knot is exactly at the spot where that reality-veil is rent at death, so that the spirit-soul can escape from the body – like a lap-dancer bursting out of a stag party cake!

One Hindu belief is that man's soul enters through the sutures of the skull, so at death it must also leave the body at that point. And if the skull doesn't burst open with the heat of the pyre, then the son performing the funeral rites has to crack it open, so the spirit doesn't remain trapped inside: 'puth' is hell and 'putra', son, is one who saves you from hell.

> [Fiona: Oh, is that why it's so important for Hindus to have a son?
> Sagarika: So they believed it was too gruesome an act for a daughter to perform?
> Promila: No, the prejudice against daughters runs much deeper.

SD: Yes. In any case, in some communities, women weren't even allowed to attend the cremation. All this is by the way, but isn't it interesting that the area on one's head where the spirit supposedly leaves the body, is where the fontanel is too? Maybe that's why hair is also so important. There are all sorts of strictures in our culture about when and how we can cut it: we sacrifice it at Tirupati temple, Sikhs don't cut it, Muslim women cover it up.

And not only in Indian belief systems: in ancient Greece, hair was substituted for sex in later vestal virgins. And it proved such a vulnerable depository for poor old Samson's strength and virility.

Sagarika: Was storytelling a male preserve?

SD: Well, only men like me wandered around telling stories, spreading our myths, legends and folktales to uneducated rustics who had no other form of entertainment.

But women were significant storytellers too, though they were confined to bed-sides – or more likely they told their tales to children sleeping next to them on the floor. Cradles and cots were for the wealthier. Most babies were left in hammocks made from old saris, slung from any high vantage point in their one-room dwellings.

Babies thus stayed in a foetal position, they couldn't straighten their legs or arms. Modern paediatrics pronounce this to be a good thing: the baby feels secure in womb-like conditions.

Well, it's certainly better than swaddling a baby: the very thought is enough to trigger a panic attack! I feel claustrophobic just to think of being tightly bound, unable to move my arms or legs. Guarantees straight limbs? More likely a guarantee to put the infant in a straitjacket later in life!

Ah yes, babies; it brings me to my story – at last, you say.]

1

My story is about Devaki, a deva-dasi, servant of god. 'Agamas', rules governing temple worship, stipulate that dance and music are necessary ingredients of daily ritual. The devadasi institution was a way of life with its own 'vritti', professional ethic, though over the centuries the devadasi accrued many categories, so that a girl dedicated to a temple could be anything from a symbolic wife to dancer to glorified prostitute to servile menial. But, to tweak Donne, there is a whole world out there, so this story is not only about Devaki. It is also about an India of two parallel worlds, the native and the Raj, and when the twain did meet.

The ayah in that photograph was Kamala, married to Velu, the mali, both working in the Smythe household in Madras. While the nineteenth century wound down, Devaki was born to Kamala in a small town in the Madras Presidency. Kamala was a typically Dravidian beauty: her large lustrous eyes, full mouth and abundant long hair offset her lack of Aryan fairness and height. Her nose was uncharacteristically small and pert, rather than broad and flat. Her narrow waist was well-defined in her otherwise ample figure; that her tiny ankles and feet supported such fullness lent even more allure to the whole.

Velu was wiry and small boned and his dark skin was further burnt during his hours under the hot sun. He perhaps cultivated his moustache to counter any meekness his less than heroic stature suggested. It was disconcerting when his nostrils flared under his steady gaze, giving him the dangerous stillness of a stalking animal.

Anthony was the older of the Smythe children. Moira Smythe's first child was a girl but the infant died of typhoid when she was weaned off the breast, probably due to infected milk. By the time Moira was pregnant again and Elaine was born, Anthony's ayah, now arthritic and wheezy, had retired to her home town, and sent Kamala as ayah for the new baby. Kamala's parents were finding it difficult to amass dowries for their four girls, so they seized the opportunity to send their youngest to the big city to earn money. There was little employment in small towns, even for men; females had few prospects for well-paid work.

Kamala had no prior experience as an ayah and her youth and attractiveness might have been a handicap in bringing up a male child but she had, after all, only to raise a girl. As to experience as an ayah: in an Indian household, there are usually babies and children of various ages whom the older girls have to look after. Bringing up a baby was a task as natural as tending cattle. It was not the daunting step that it is now in the West, needing advice and guidance from books and social workers.

[Akhil: Well, that gives them grounds to sue someone if things go wrong!
SD: Spoken like a true American lawyer!]

###

Velu had grown up in the Smythe household. His father, Perumal, first came to work in Madras after the severe drought and famine that struck much of South India in 1877, killing over five million people. The Presidency had already suffered such pestilence in 1818, believed to be a part of the widespread weather-fallout from Tombora's volcanic eruption in 1815. Most agriculturists were forced to abandon their lands to seek work and food further afield. [Doesn't the word "afield" suggest that all men were once agriculturists? Yes, I'm a lexophile and can't resist etymological asides. Since I sew words together, I should also be allowed to unpick them!]. These peasants ended up begging in towns.

Not only did Viceroy Lord Lytton not implement available relief measures during the Great Famine of

1876-78, he continued to export record amounts of grain to Britain. Equally iniquitous, landowners and farmers in Bengal Presidency were forced to abandon food crops to grow poppy for opium to seduce the recalcitrant Chinese into trade submission. After such famines, the British authorities turned their attention to improving the water situation in the Indian areas they governed. One acre in every seven was irrigated, with 17 million acres watered by canals built and maintained by the government. For a population of 300 million agriculturists, such boasts of irrigation projects were double-edged: often water dues were imposed, and in some cases the revenue assessments on land were increased to pay for the new improvements.

Yes, the British government invested $1,750,000,000 capital for India's commercial and industrial development, but India only reaped spillover benefits from this statistic, by way of employment for its people. India was the largest producer of food and raw material in the Empire. Britain's import of wheat, meal and flour from India, exceeded those from Canada and doubled those from Australia.

Yes, the British introduced tea and jute into India, but as valuable plantation crops, not to satisfy the native population's needs. They also laid 25,000 miles of railway and 100,000 miles of telegraph wire but these, too, were not as wholly altruistic as its historians would have us believe. Good communication and speedy transportation were needed for goods being exported or imported.

And, the shadow of the Mutiny still upon them, swift movement of troops was also crucial.

We still enjoy remnants of those communication systems and water resources, but successive Indian governments have not done enough to develop, or even merely to maintain them in proportion to our population explosion. Things are no different now for the Indian farmer; he is still at the mercy of rain, still to be seen squatting on his haunches, ruminating on his wad of tobacco, looking skywards – though instead of Indra's rain-clouds, he most often sees Vritra (adversary of Indra and personification of drought) mocking him from the blistering blue.

Velu had often heard his parents talk of that drought in their village, how displaced families roamed far, willing to do any work for a mouthful of food, how children were sold into bondage for a measure of rice. Though the East India Company had banned slavery, sale of children during famine was exempt.

Perumal recalled the drought that dislocated them:

- Our hearts shrivelled with the standing crops and our stomachs soon followed. We villagers had lived amicably for decades, but now we fought over water in the wells and tanks. Do you remember, Valli, how our beloved cow collapsed, too exhausted even to drink the bucket of water I had scraped from the tank? It was too muddy for human consumption, but soon even we were drinking that. Such despair that we would be driven out of the security of our land – if one survived. So many died, that the souls must have clung to Yama's buffalo like tics.

Tears came to his wife, Valli, whenever they talked of their home. She said of their neighbour:

- He was such a nice, quiet man, how did he go mad like that? I can still hear his wife's screams and the children's cries of anguish. We rushed over and found he was shouting madly, hitting out at anyone who went near him. Your father ran and brought the 'valluvan', we thought he was possessed, and he needed the exorcist.
- But Valli, the 'valluvan' confirmed what I felt, that he wasn't bewitched. Yes, I know he wasn't acting normally, such a gentle and serene man. I think he just went berserk, seeing his fields in ruination, his life withered.

Perumal was not far wrong: so well established is the desperation when one is divorced from one's land that the word delirium comes from the Latin "delirare": he who turns away from his furrow. It was a bitter wrench for Perumal, forced to leave his wife and infant son with his paltry savings and the little rice that was stored in the earthenware jar. Fortunately he finally found employment in Madras with the Smythes and sent for his family to join him, though his land remained a burr lodged in his memory. Ownership of his plot of land had given them a reasonable living when weather conditions were favourable. More importantly, they had independence and the security of an established community. But in his pragmatic way, Perumal could see that village grass wasn't necessarily greener when viewed from the city. He had seen too many farmers in perpetual debt as crops, ever at the mercy of weather and disease, could not meet taxes on the land, land that they often no longer owned.

> [Bhaumi: But it's no different now. NGOs are still fighting against bonded labour.
> Advik: I agree. I'm here to research Indian agriculture and I'm appalled how little conditions have changed.]

The community also had caste obligations they dared not defy: dowry for the daughter, prescribed funeral rites, new clothes at festivals, jewellery and expenses at weddings, priests' fees ... perennial debt. But farmers stoically persevered, knowing no life other than that under an unrelenting sun, moneylenders bearing down on them as mercilessly.

Though Perumal was not a gardener by caste, he soon reconciled himself to his demotion as a mali. Working the earth and tending cows allowed him to feel at least some of that bucolic peace he had left behind, instead of turning into a mere city lackey. A couple of weeks convinced Perumal that, with hard work and frugality, he could earn and save some money for ... well, who knew what the future would bring. The important thing was that he could send for his wife and young son, Velu, to join him.

###

Moira Smythe, the doraisani, maintained a garden, as did all British memsahibs.

> [Rishab: What was that word?
> SD: Right, I'll be using some Tamil words. Translations: "dorai" is the sahib and "doraisani" the memsahib. "Chinna-dorai" is junior sahib or baba, and "doraimār" are white people.
> When they are referred to as "vellakāran" or "parangi", it is with disdain, as north Indians would use "firangi" or "mleccha".]

Where was I? Yes, Moira's garden. The driveway divided the desultory lawn into two semi-circles, hedged with plumbago. Whenever Perumal saw those little flowers, their faded blue reminded him of the doraisani's eyes, similarly sad and washed out. Flowers hardy enough to withstand the harsh climate grew in a regimental arrangement of pots: phlox, geraniums, salvia, balsam, begonias, even roses. This made for a portable garden, necessary for those who got posted to various places; their potted plants just travelled with the rest of the baggage. Sturdier hibiscus dotted the lawn and variegated croton bushes flanked the wall; these were planted into the ground, the plants too large to be transported. Morning glory and flowering creepers trailed over arches, while bougainvillea smothered the compound walls with splashes of colour, alleviating the drab prospect.

[Compound: the word's original meaning is "to combine"; but its colonial application denoted a walled enclosure, probably a mispronunciation of the Malay "kampong".]

While watering the garden, Perumal would often recall his crops wilting in that merciless devastation; there seemed no shortage of water to keep *this* vast garden going, though it struggled against the heat. Ferns were also cultivated, to lend delicate tracery to Moira's flower arrangements. Though Mr Smythe stiffened in protest when he heard Moira calling one maidenhair, insisting she use its Latin name instead – though, unfortunately, she could never remember that.

Moira would have loved a kitchen garden to grow "English vegetables" that were not available at the local market, but they did well only in the higher reaches of the Nilgiris. Friends who had been up to Ooty would sometimes bring down delicacies like artichokes, asparagus, rhubarb ... Moira now considered even the lowly Brussel sprouts a treat, though she had scorned them in England.

###

Velu grew up in the huge compound, which had quarters at one end, to house servants. Their distance ensured that noisy declarations of Indian ablutions and domestic quarrels, and "those dreadful smells" of latrines and native spices, would not reach the bungalow. There were also stables for horses, and two cows that Perumal offered to look after. After the Symthe baby died of typhoid, a fresh unadulterated supply of milk for the children was essential.

Velu's mother, Valli, could not forget the life she had had to abandon. She was shocked that Perumal had demeaned himself with this job:

- Yén-gō, you're a mali now?! Haven't they asked you yet to go and cure small pox? Yes Velu, in our villages the mali is Goddess Mariamma's priest.

  You are a 'vellāla', an agriculturist. No matter how small your plot of land was, it was yours. Chee, you are not mali caste.

For all his phlegmatic son-of-the-soil demeanour, Perumal was equal to Valli's jibes:

- Pōhn-gō, don't you know the proverb, "This is the law of my caste, and this is the law of my belly"? You have to adapt, woman. When we get back to our village, who will know what I've been doing here? And, don't worry, everywhere money always talks louder than jāthi-vāthi.
- But you are looking after cows like a 'kōnan'!
- Āhahā, my clever woman, a kōnan looks after sheep, not cows. Unless you are promoting me to a king? Oh my dear wife, don't you know, Kō means king ...?

Āhahā, so that you can be a queen or what? Or are you elevating me even further? Kō is also god, king of heaven, that is why he lives in a 'kō-il'.

- King-ā, god-ā?! 'Yénna paittiyam', such madness! You're just a mali and cowherd now. Pōhn-gō, father of Velu, everything always turned into a joke.
- Yén-gō, mother of Velu, what is wrong in looking after cows? Didn't our Lord Krishna do it? Yén-gō, *who* loves pure fresh milk, butter and ghee so much that in the village we had to keep our own cow, uh? *You*, not your kōnan husband! And when you are dying, we will put a cow's tail in your hand so that it can lead you to heaven!

Valli spat to negate the mention of death.

- Thoo thoo, don't you dare talk about me dying!
- Séri, very well then, you give *me* its tail when I'm ...
- Chee, you stop all such inauspicious talk right now! Āhahā, you think because of your name you've become a big man eh? Don't you know Velu, Pérumāl is the same as 'périya-āl': "big man" indeed, huh, when you have to salaam that boss mali of yours, though he's of a lower caste! And you've even cut off your vellāla 'kudumī'!
- That's because I don't want you pulling it every time you're angry with me! I don't need any caste signs. After all, doesn't our proverb compare the vellāla with the brinjal, because both will mix palatably with anything? I've put food in our stomachs, now I want

to save up enough money to go back to my land. That is all I want. And you don't help. If you also worked, we would have enough money to go back before next year's planting season.

- Yén-gō, you casteless wonder, just because I'm your wife, I haven't become an 'ādimai', a serf. *Me*, subordinate myself to those *pariahs* Agnes and Francis …? Āhahā, you who are so fond of our proverbs, haven't you heard *my* favourite? "Chappals are to be worn on the *feet*; don't put them on your *head*"!

Valli could have been employed in the Smythes' kitchen as a skivvy who ground spices, washed pots and pans, cleaned rice and dhal, and as a "tunny ketch" [fetching water: 'tunny'= water, and ketch was probably a corruption of catch]. But she was horrified at the mere suggestion. However, she swept and cleaned their own quarters, fetched water and kept their brass pots shining. In the little yard at the back of their house, Perumal planted flowers for her puja and chaplet for her hair, and culinary plants – coriander and mint, drumsticks, chillies and curry leaves – things she had grown in their backyard in the village.

Velu hung around his father whenever it was not too hot to help water the plants or relieve Perumal of backbreaking weeding. Later, when the senior mali died and Perumal took his place, Velu became full-time assistant and found pruning, grafting and repotting came easily to him. He also helped his father look after the docile cows, and monopolised the task of feeding them. Perumal loved them, saying they reminded him of the kine he had in his village; he would often talk with such sadness about the place. He would sluice the cows with water, making a shooooosh sound while he rubbed them down. Indian villagers susurrate when dealing with anything liquid: they emit a similar hiss when bathing children, or when they encourage infants to urinate. Velu would tease his father that he loved these beasts more than he did his son, for when Perumal felt particularly affectionate, he would ruffle Velu's hair and call him "my little calf".

###

It can be said that Anthony and Velu grew up together, yet apart: the lakshman rekha was very clearly established, for all its invisibility. Velu hadn't even ventured as far as the porch steps. Once, when Perumal was about to take cut flowers to the doraisani, he heard a cow lowing, seemingly in distress. Velu picked up the flowers which Perumal had left on the balustrade and ran up two steps, intending to put them in the shade of the veranda, only to be met by the bearer Joseph, who snatched them from him and told him never to set foot thus far again.

Anthony found in Velu, who was a few years older, a convenient makeshift to alleviate his boredom. As Anthony was interested only in batting, he could summon Velu to play cricket, getting him to bowl and field. Or when Moira found time and energy to knock a few tennis balls around with Anthony, there was Velu to retrieve errant balls – plenty of those, since mother and son were barely competent players.

When the baba dorai, Anthony and Elaine, came into the garden to play, Velu found joining them was a good excuse for him to abandon his tasks, but he would quietly retreat when the children were called for tea, served on the veranda. The baba-dorai did not share their biscuits, cakes and sandwiches with the servants' children. It was "Just not done. Those children don't expect it. Besides, who knows what their caste nonsense dictates what they can and can't eat. And it might even be a caste offence for them to accept food from us – the cheek of it!"

For all that indoctrination, Elaine would feel an unnamed uneasiness in not treating Velu as they did their neighbours, the Wilson children. It seemed against the Christian charity and compassion their church sermons enjoined. There were many such unexplained aspects of their life in India, but they were programmed to live unquestioningly by the rules.The Smythe parents had drummed it into them that unfathomable caste rules operated on both sides of the divide. After all, the Raj's keeping up of appearances was but an approved echo of the strict form and protocol that ruled Hindu castes.

The Wilsons had three children, the older boy Edward already in boarding school in England. William Wilson trailed Anthony like a devoted spaniel but was too young to be a real companion, though Anthony out of boredom would sometimes deign to knock a cricket ball around with him – as long as William did all the fielding. When Anthony tired of him, William would read, or play draughts and ludo with the girls. Though he missed his brother Edward, he wasn't looking forward to joining him in the English boarding school he'd been sent to a few years ago.

Anne Wilson, an ardent follower of local culture, thought it more important for her children to accompany her on her "expeditions", so her children's primary home schooling was sketchy at best, as William found to his cost when he entered mainstream schooling, though his unorthodox early education paid rich dividends when he went up to Oxford. Jane, being the same age as Elaine, was her constant companion – but they were *girls*! So, by default, Anthony had often to turn to Velu.

Velu taught Anthony how to negotiate the difficult branches of trees and where to find the nest of a particular egg Anthony wanted to add to his collection. He showed him which sapling was supple enough to cut to bend into a native bow, from which clay balls were shot at marauding monkeys and insolent crows. Velu's shots invariably found their mark and the canny crows learned to stay away when they saw this weapon in his hand, but if the younger boy was using it, they continued to hop with temerity closer to the food on the veranda. When Anthony got his first popgun, he refused to let Velu touch it: now he'd show him a thing or two about scaring pests away!

Anthony resented it when Velu won at marbles,

how he ignored his bleeding fingers while manipulating manja during kite fights and, with a well-aimed hit with his spinning top, could cleave a rival's. Unlike Anthony, Elaine saw no rival in Velu, and despite her brother's scoffing, she delighted in the little doll Velu made with a wooden clothes peg. He picked a picotee and carefully sliced off the calyx. He inserted the peg through the upside-down bloom so that the round peg emerged like a head. The pretty lemon-coloured carnation, delicately edged with red, was like a ballerina's tutu around the two wooden peg legs. He stuck the calyx tip on the head as a jaunty cap, and drew in the face with a bit of charcoal.

Velu had dealt with a range of practical contingencies that made him dexterous and resourceful, resulting in Anthony's grudging envy. He also had the sort of freedom children envy: no school or lessons, no strict nursery rules, and his clothing – baggy khaki shorts, loose banian and going barefoot – gave him unrestricted movement, whereas Anthony was bound* by George Smythe's rule of "always being on show in front of the natives", condoning neither loosening of "character" considerations nor sartorial strictures.

"Setting an example to the ruled" was paramount. Memsahibs no less jealously guarded the social fabric, as starchy as their skirts. Strict hierarchy was established not only to ensure the status quo of the Raj way of life, but also to protect their personal standing in that pecking order. That stiff backbone supported Raj morals, the only guarantee of achievement of character against this country's demoralisation that, like the heat, could seep into one's bones – and worse, into men's nether parts. Shameful how some of their menfolk lowered the ruling status by forming liaisons with native women! That was common among the native men, who referred to their mistresses as 'chinna-veeda', their "little houses" or "second homes". But surely Englishmen could see how inferior these native women were, surely not worth maintaining as their "keeps" – or, as a boxwallah would euphemistically announce, "I'm visiting my Branch Office today!"

Well-schooled in Raj directives, Anthony found in them the perfect excuse to conceal the ambivalent admiration he felt for Velu. Christmas was the perfect time to rub in their differences. When Anthony showed Velu his most prized present, a fine penknife, he saw the longing in Velu's eyes. Velu immediately shimmied up the albeezia tree and lopped off a suitable branch with his 'mandé-katthi', a hatchet Anthony was forbidden to use. As Anthony fumbled trying to whittle a spinning top out of the soft wood, Velu was itching to take the penknife from him: he could show him how to do it, oh the things he could do with that knife! With spiteful delight, Anthony deprived him of that pleasure.

Weeks later, when Anthony tired of his clumsy attempts with the penknife, he let Velu use it. Out of the wood Anthony had abandoned, Velu carved a horse, stiff and stylised, like the terracotta horses he had seen standing outside villages, and shyly presented it to Anthony. Months later, Velu found his gift thrown in the garden; perhaps Anthony had to abandon such vestiges of his early boyhood before leaving for boarding school.

2

On Anthony's first holiday from boarding school at Home – the weather and its people equally cold and punishing – he was glad of the warmth and joyous freedom of this other home. It was so good to be waited on by adoring servants, with Francis making his favourite dishes. He didn't have to wait his turn to have a bath after the seniors had wallowed in the water, he didn't have to make his bed, polish his shoes, or clear at table. These chores, though minor, had added to his misery in boarding school with its discipline, rules, prefects to obey, boys to fend off or negotiate with.

Velu was now too busy as assistant mali to spend much time with Anthony, who was surprised to find that he missed Velu's company; previously, it was so much his to command. Mornings were boring for Anthony, with the Wilson children having lessons with their mother, while Elaine had a tutor. Moira was not going to send her delicate daughter away to school. Boys had to go, that was taken for granted, but Moira clung to her beautiful Elaine. She did not want to lose her to a cold distance, having ensured her survival even in this disease-ridden hot country. The young Miss Woods was inexperienced but was needed initially only for Elaine's grounding in the 3 R-s. She had come off the boat but a month ago and, Moira suspected, was part of the Fishing Fleet. Fortunately, Miss Woods was rather plain, not likely to be snapped up in a hurry by any eager bachelor, and that was sufficient assurance that Miss Woods was likely to continue teaching Elaine for some time.

When Elaine's morning studies were over, she most often went over to Jane's, Anthony accompanying her if he had nothing better to do. He hated it when the boys would be roped in to play fathers at dolls' tea parties, the prospect of cook Ramu's small sandwiches, miniature cakes and biscuits being the only compensation for Anthony's squirming attendance.

Or the girls would take their dolls on a picnic, though eating outdoors was stopped when a kite swooped down and snatched a sandwich from Elaine's hand, while Kamala was rather preoccupied eyeing Velu's naked torso. Scavenging kites, not content with raking over rubbish tips, could spot such easy targets with their famous aerial vision.

- Ayah, Jane is coming to play with Elaine. See that they stay in the shade and don't let them take off their hats or shoes.

The girls loved the gulmohar tree that bloomed an orange blaze in May. They would pick the fallen flowers, pull off the sepals and assiduously separate the green and red layers. They would lick their fingernails, then carefully stick the pointed ovals on them. A conversation ensued, in imitation of their mothers, with much gesticulation to show off their long carmine fingernails. Or, again mimicking their mothers, they would pretend to sit at a dressing table – which held such fascination for little girls, with its battery of lipsticks, fragrant creams and assorted bottles of perfume – and powder their faces with the pink flowers of the rain tree, soft and fluffy as the powder puffs their mothers used, but much more tickly.

The garden yielded other subjects for their imagination:

- Let's pick these shoe-flowers.
- What a funny name for them. They don't look like shoes.
- I think their proper name is hi-biscuit. Maybe they're called shoe flowers because they're used to polish shoes.
- Let's try them on our shoes.

After their attempts, Elaine and Jane got up off their haunches and shook out their dresses.

- Ayyō missy-ma, what you done?! Got red red on your dress, Yellen-missy! What I telling doraisani? She ask me why I not looking when you doing.

Kamala could well feel guilty: she was too busy flirting with Velu to pay much attention to the missies. Kamala struck her forehead with the flat of her hand, a characteristic gesture of despair.

- Ayyō, doraisani be too too angry.

###

While some natives had such problems, their white superiors had their share as well. Witness the doraisani: Moira is recumbent on her chaise longue, her attention only intermittently given to the morning post or library book. Agnes has released doraisani's heat-swollen feet from the tyranny of shoes and Moira indulges in the luxury of having her feet massaged. Agnes, her personal ayah, is something in the nature of a lady's maid, who sets out her ironed clothes, jerks her into her stays, laces her shoes and helps dress her hair. The lament at the Club was, "Such an awful deprivation in this country, the non-availability of a proper lady's hairdresser!" Though the Madras memsahibs could be grateful that they did not have to succumb to the barber's scissors to get their hair cut, as did the muffasil memsahibs.

The awful heat sanctioned an afternoon nap but an unnamed unease prevented Moira from dozing off. The feeling of stagnation never left her, though the weather was blamed: not even a breeze to stir one to some worthwhile activity. Though there was so little to do, even that seemed to sap her energy. Her daily domestic routine was unvarying. After bed tea and those delicious small bananas that kept them "regular", Moira looked forward to their morning rides, glad of the couple of hours with her husband. In the evenings, he was usually sequestered in his library, occupied with papers or some reading – "a compulsory part of my job, dear" – though she suspected another reason was that side table, always set out with drinks.

She then made her post-breakfast rounds of the house, checking that everything had been dusted, the brass and plate polished. Well, at least she no longer had to do the dhobi account. Fortunately, after Reginald heard at the Club that Enid's children had got dreadful dhobi itch, he agreed to convert one of the stables into another quarter where they now had a resident washerman. One was never sure how clean the water was in which dhobis washed clothes. And it was said that they often hired out white sheets as table cloths!

The kitchen was Moira's main area of operation: ordering meals, checking the storeroom and making a list of provisions needed, which would give her an excuse to go shopping; those items from the bazaar she would, of course, leave to Francis. Oh, he made his cut; they all did, and the problems with servants was a constant topic of ladies' conversations, when they left the men after dinner. Or at the Club where they met for coffee, while eagerly seeking the latest fashions and London news in magazines that were already weeks old. Not that fashion mattered, as every other lady would be wearing London's last season's dresses, run up by skilful native tailors.

Moira was unable to overcome the guilt that accompanied her life of idleness. She was aware that other wives shrugged off their unproductive lives, having decided happily to enjoy all the creature comforts as compensation for the sacrifices they were making to live in this infernal place. She even envied the frivolous regimental wives, with their lively Mess functions. It might have been the proverbial grass being greener on the other side of the fence, but she felt those gatherings would be far more interesting than the boring formal dinners attended by the same set of people and invariably being seated next to the same person, so rigid was rank that governed table placement.

The alienation she felt in this country was exacerbated by an unnamed loneliness that Club gatherings and the social hum could not blot out. Even her darling Elaine could not fill that chilly hiatus between her and Reginald, though he also doted on his daughter.

###

Elaine thrived as her parents' favourite and it was a source of surprise to Anne Wilson that she had not become spoiled or precious, though Jane had often to exert herself whenever Elaine was bossy, trying to have her way. Anthony was neither impressed nor interested in their preoccupations:

- Look at these dolls my Selvi-ayah brought me from her village.
- Dolls? They look more like logs, all stiff and straight.

Jane, who knew much more about such native matters, indignantly protested:

- Well Anthony, they are wooden man and woman dolls that Indian children play with.
- Well I think they're silly. They don't have proper arms and legs that can move. And they're so dull: they don't even have eyes or hair. All the same horrible brown.

But Anthony's scorn couldn't dampen the girls' enthusiasm.

- We can paint their eyes in.
- And make hair out of black string – a long plait would be nice. Agnes-ayah can sew them nice clothes. She can make a shiny sari for her and a turban for him. Let's dress them up like bride and groom and we can have their wedding! All our dolls will attend dressed in their best clothes.
- They are my dolls, Elaine, so I'll choose. They'll wear what Tamil children wear.

Thwarted, Elaine stalked off with Anthony but he knew the girls would soon be back together again. So it went in those carefree days, chafed only with such nursery skirmishes, the heat and scritchy underwear. Time hung as heavy as the heat. In the afternoons they were confined to playing in the darkened gloom of their nursery with toys, rocking horses and anything else parents could lay their hands on to keep their children entertained, if not usefully occupied.

The girls pressed flowers they'd collected into books. Jane had taken the heaviest book she could find in her parents' extensive library and put phlox between pages. Her mother was very cross when she found the pages of a valuable first edition had been stained. To avoid a repetition of that, Mrs Wilson showed the girls how to put the flowers between tissue paper and cardboard, then weigh them down with books. Of an afternoon, Jane and Elaine would examine their collections: which flowers had faded, which best kept their colour. They would make cards, pasting the dried flowers on kindergarten card, pink blue yellow. That required a trifle more attention than getting all the wrinkles out of silver-paper chocolate wrappers by rubbing them with a smooth pebble, the shiny flat results which they saved in an album, giving them much satisfaction.

"Quiet time" was boring. The boys were forced to keep their usual boisterousness in check. If they had no new magazines to read, they would whittle with their penknives, play with trains or compare their stamp collections to see which duplicates could be swopped, raring to be set free in the garden after tea, when the sun had lost its fierceness. The boys were in their element outdoors, climbing trees, blowing whistles, banging drums. Their toy pistols with "red-caps" produced the most satisfying bang, scaring the mongoose or 'anil', the Indian chipmunk. Croquet had been installed on the lawn but Anthony was too good for the younger children; it was a treat when his parents joined him for a game after tea. He enjoyed a pre-breakfast ride with his parents in the park near the Race Course. Despite the ranging deer, it was possible to have a good gallop instead of merely trotting around their compound.

The Symthe children were sometimes taken to the Club to play with other children while their parents played tennis. It was also a treat because they could have tea in the Club, before being sent home, while their parents stayed on for the tea dance or bridge. Anthony looked forward to his tennis coaching three afternoons a week and the company of other boys who, like him, were home on holiday. Cricket on the dusty maidans was not as enjoyable as playing it in England – one couldn't throw oneself about on the outfield as one could on those grassy fields.

###

However, the Smythe parents did not socialise with their Wilson neighbours. They reluctantly let the children do so, for lack of other company, though Reginald Smythe disapproved of Elaine getting too close to Jane.

When Elaine excitedly reported,

- Daddy, Jane's ayah gave her such a funny little doll! He had a smiley elephant face but a man's body, with a big tummy, and sitting on a rat! Can Joseph get me one from the bazaar?

it further justified his reservations:

- Moira, I wouldn't have our Elaine going around too often to the Wilsons'. They're far too interested in things native.

  That "doll" she talked about is obviously an idol; they celebrated that Ganeysher festival recently. Worshipping an elephant, I ask you!
- It's because Madame Anne fancies herself an intellectual. She even went to university I think! You should see their library! And she's aiming to get Edward into Oxford.

  She's the one interested in local customs. She even allows the children to run around barefoot and half-dressed! And they call their servants by name! I only call Agnes that to distinguish her from the other ayah, Kamala.
- Well, some of that's rubbed off on our Georgie. Odd fish the pair of them. Kitchen Tamil's not good enough, they have a Brahmin in to teach them Tamil and Sanskrit. Much good that'll do him with his coolies, who best understand a couple of well-aimed kicks!

- Yes, they don't really lead the typical life enjoyed by the rest of the boxwallahs.
- He doesn't work for a Company, Moira. He owns his business! But still "Trade". Pedlars, whether itinerant or millionaires! Third generation, so thinks he knows everything about this country and considers us only birds of passage.
- But they shouldn't let the side down. She's been heard to express some very unsavoury views. She said it's demeaning to make servants take off our shoes and have them dress us and ....
- Why can't these cavilling bleeding hearts see that servants have always done all that for their rajas! And they are used to being treated like scum by their Brahmins, so it's really only a carry-over of their caste system, not something we have introduced! They *expect* us to exert our superiority, much as they expect it of their caste superiors.
- I suppose the Wilsons can afford to break the rules because of their money and their beautiful home!
- Well, they live permanently in their own house so don't have to cart their chattel around. What do you expect when we get posted all over the place, having to move no sooner than we feel settled somewhere? We don't want to have our personal things getting damaged in transit. You know how heartbroken you were when your mother's crystal vase broke.

But we'll look forward to a grand retirement, shall we, our own house in England, with our own things.

And don't you forget, if he's not exactly a boxwallah, he's still only a little better than your chinaman who comes around with his tin trunk, tempting you with his silks and embroidered linen spread out on the veranda.

- Oh, yesterday I bought the most darling little embroidered dress from Ching Chong ....
- Yes yes dear ... point is, the Wilsons are not top drawer, not only because they have connections in commerce, but because of the way they carry on. It's usually the other way around: those in trade are interested in nothing but money, and show no interest in natives, except as a work force.

###

The Wilsons' appraisal of the Smythes was expressed with less rancour.

- Oh George, Moira made such a fuss that I gave Elaine that sweet little Ganesha! "We want none of those heathen idols in our home, thenk-kyew very much!" And she was horrified that our children eat dosais with their fingers. I told her they couldn't be eaten with a knife and fork, no more than custard can be eaten with one's fingers!
- Wasn't she appalled that they're even allowed to eat dosais? Isn't it awful when conventions trap an ingrown community with such trivialities ... and oh the pretentiousness: Smythe?! I'm sure he's just

plain old Smith! And do you know he won't have anyone call him Reg? And Reggie, heaven forbid! I'm surprised their children are allowed to play with ours.

- I'm not. Moira loves her card sessions so our children are tolerable because they speak English. Those Smythe children always want company, they hardly read.
- Don't their parents read to them? I suppose he's far too busy, stiff with official work. You know, it's put about that he's a bit too fond of the bottle; probably needs it to unbend. .

By the way, unfortunately I think our new man, Raju, has the same weakness!

- Here's another strange contradiction I've found with Hindus. The ocean is considered so polluting that anyone crossing the Black Water has to undergo purification ceremonies. The same proscription about any liquid doesn't allow them to drink water from each other's wells. But they'll quite happily help themselves to your Glenlivet!

Oh, there's Elaine now. I am fond of her though she can be iron-willed, under that porcelain prettiness! She's bright, if only she'd get more encouragement. Certainly brighter than that bully, Anthony.

###

Anthony wasn't above eliciting Elaine's support when he wanted a puppy. It would be such fun teaching their puppy tricks, how to shake hands, roll over on its back, sit when it was told to, like the one the House Master in England had. He wouldn't be so bored if he could play with a puppy, making it retrieve a ball or stick in this vast garden. But their father adamantly refused, knowing the risk of rabies. And, for once, their mother didn't soften to her son's pestering either: after battling so many of the diseases and illnesses this country could throw at one, she dreaded inviting one more into her home. In fact, just before the holidays, Moira had a scare.

Elaine was running a very high fever and consulting that medical Bible, *Dr Moore's Family Medicine*, did not help. The surgeon was called in but Moira wasn't satisfied with his diagnosis or, rather, the lack of it. He couldn't say exactly what it was; it could be malaria, it would have to be monitored. Elaine lay inert in her bed, Kamala refusing to leave her post at its foot. She suggested:

- Someone's bad eye on Yellen-missy. Doraisani, I do dhristi. She come well then.

In desperation, Moira allowed what she would normally have termed native mumbo-jumbo. Kamala loosened some sticks from the broom, lit them and circled them around the listless child, as Moira had seen a temple priest do with camphor fire in front of the idol. Kamala waved the fire out, pretended to spit on it and then put a spot of the black ash on Elaine's cheek.

When Reginald looked in on his daughter that evening, he saw the black smudge.

- What's this then? Been up the chimney, have you?
- Silly Daddy. We don't have chimneys in Madras!
- You were in the kitchen then, watching Francis making your favourite macaroons?
- No, I don't feel like eating at all.
- I'll get Logan to bring you some Ovaltine shall I? Got to keep up your strength.
- Daddy, Mrs Wilson said we shouldn't be calling him Logan, that his name is *Lō-ga-nā-than*.
- Pshaw, we've just shortened it. Easier on the tongue if we leave out all those suffixes: nāthan sāmee aiyā …. Bad enough we have to remember their first names! Or should we just call him Nathan, good old Biblical name! Goodnight darling.

Reginald was not sanguine when he asked Moira about it over dinner:

- Really Moira, that black spot! Next ayah will be plastering your forehead with cow-dung to cure your megrim. Do you think her hocus-pocus is going to make the slightest bit of difference?

But the anxious mother was only hedging her bets. She couldn't tell him that, having lost her first baby girl, she couldn't bear the thought of Elaine being taken as well. Reginald could scoff at the evil eye but it was true, Elaine was a beautiful child. The native women marvelled at her blue eyes, fair curls and rosy cheeks that they pinched with affection if they got a chance. And feeling guilty for their expressed admiration, would immediately make a circling motion with their hands around Elaine's head and then crack their knuckles against their temples, a more instantaneous way to scare off evil spirits.

###

Perumal's dream of returning to his village was never realised, for he died of mouth cancer, just short of the money he needed to reclaim his land. House servants were forbidden the "disgusting habit" of chewing tobacco, but because Perumal worked outdoors, his addiction to the pernicious practice was unimpeded. But this inadvertent dispensation took a premature toll on him. Already embittered at her loss of status, life without her husband made Valli even more rootless. The sin of being a widow was too much for her:

- I shouldn't continue staying among these parangis. I should shave my head and do penance at some thīrthā.

[Promila: "Widow's penance?!" Those pilgrimage centres like Benares and Vrindavan are nothing but frozen sati!
Sagarika: I agree. Ghastly widows' homes; nothing holy about them.
Fiona: But what alternatives did that generation of women have – if at all they were given a choice?].

Velu promised his mother that they would return to their village. With his promotion to Perumal's position, he would soon earn the balance money. But Valli died shortly after, having lost the will to live. Velu was on his own. The community catchment was absent here: no relatives who would feed him, or matchmaker to find him a wife.

He was a natural target for Kamala's wiles. She made herself a sympathetic companion, though well within the bounds of propriety. Kamala normally ate with the other servants. Servants' food was cooked in an outhouse by the skivvy, for Francis was too grand for that; he was the *family* cook. Of course, when Valli was alive, she wouldn't let Perumal or Velu eat food cooked by anyone else, leave alone by a pariah; she always cooked for her family. The knowing Kamala now started cooking for Velu, as if further to underline her awareness of his needs.

Kamala's mother periodically sent her marriage proposals, pressurising her to marry. But Kamala liked city life and wanted to stay on in Madras, and saw her opportunity in Velu. Here was a desirable boy, for there was that nice little stash Perumal had set aside! True, Velu was a bit short, dark and slight but then, most Tamilians were. But from a 'valangai', right-handed-caste, as Valli never failed to remind anyone who would listen, particularly those pariahs, Francis and Agnes, who thought themselves so superior just because they were Christians!

###

By the time Anthony came on his next vacation, with ephebic eruptions of acne and testosterone, Velu had married Kamala.

- Did I tell you, Reginald, the ayah and mali want to get married. I suppose that means they'll want leave for the wedding. Terrible nuisance that, two servants going off at the same time.
- I am sure the others will stand in for them. They can cope, lord knows there are enough of them hanging around … This mutton's a bit tough, dear.
- Oh Velu is not the problem, anyone can water the garden, but Elaine is really attached to her ayah. A bit of a minx really, is our Kamala, the way she's got the child so dependent on her.
- Come come, Moira, that's hardly fair. She seems genuinely to be fond of Elaine – and it leaves you free for your social whirl.
- Hmmm, I wonder how many days off they'll want. And they're sure to want an advance. Quite shocking how much they are willing to spend on their weddings, even getting into debt with the 'chettys' to maintain their social prestige.
- Oh Moira, I forgot to tell you; Francis also wants leave. His family has built a house in his village. He's done well out of us, to be able to buy his own plot of land and build a house!
- When does he want to go? Reginald, we can't possibly give all of them leave at the same time. And it's awful to be without a cook. Why can't Francis take leave

when we go to Ooty next month?

- I doubt he'll be persuaded of that: the priest has already given them an auspicious date and time for them to "enter the house".

•

Reginald indicated the tough piece of meat on his fork, with raised eyebrows.

- The mutton? Ye-es, Francis will have to have his little arrangement with another butcher; the chops he served up last week were nothing but bone.

  But what's all this about auspicious time? I thought only Hindoos had house blessings and that these native Christians had abandoned such hocus pocus. In fact, they seem so keen on imitating us: Francis shuffling off to church, usually inebriated, in his Sunday best: the old hat, shirt, tie and trousers you gave him ....
- Oh yes, they are called rice-Christians with good reason. Embracing our religion benefits their stomachs. What amuses me is that they think they have to behave like us, to show that they are one of us, as it were. They very proudly eat meat, are given the names of our saints, parrot the Lord's Prayer in English, though they probably don't understand a word ...
- (Sniffing) ... and copy our drinking habits as well!
- Don't start on me, Moira. They've always had their country liquor, so don't tell me they've learned to drink from *us*. And if the level in the gin bottle seems unusually low, I suggest you keep an eye on Logan.

I daresay my liquor makes a wonderful change from that awful arrack he normally tipples.

As I was saying, dear, those who "Have Seen The Light" put on all these outward shows, but at heart they have never given up their caste prejudices; they still stick to their own kind, use separate wells, won't intermarry. Bad enough these heathens with all their superstitious tosh, but now the Papists are encouraging it with their flock. It's just such a pathetic attempt to give converts prestige: by retaining certain caste practices, they hope their followers feel they are as good as the brethren they deserted!

Primitive savages these natives, of whatever religious persuasion. But we can't do without them, unfortunately. We need them to make our life in this inferno tolerable.

3

When Kamala found she was pregnant, she insisted they give up their lucrative employment to rush off to her "native place", much to Velu's bewilderment.

– Why did you insist on leaving Madras in such a hurry, Kamala? I thought we'd decided to live there, where our marriage would be more acceptable? And leaving when you are in this condition? What heat! You could have had the baby there; we had nice quarters. It is so hot here. There you spent most of your time in the bungalow, so you could have been under the fan.

I used to try to get under the shade of that rain tree whenever I could, and poured buckets of water over myself when I was watering the plants, making sure no one saw me "wasting water".

- Doraisani wouldn't have kept me when I got too big to run after Yellen-missy. And after I'd had my baby, she knew I'd breast feed, so wouldn't sleep in missy's room in the night. Better we left before they asked us to. And look: she gave me some of missy's baby clothes.
- Huh, what good are they? We will have a *son*. In any case, our baby doesn't need these kind of clothes; it would die of heat in them! These doraimār still haven't learned how to dress for this country.

The topi was the outward item of the English person's compulsory clothing. Unseen was the flannel or wool worn next to the skin. A Manual, advising the family going out to India, stipulates: "Woollen clothing, thick or thin, should be the clothing of a child all the year round".

- And what's this 'pōtō', Kamala?
- I wanted a 'pōtō' of Yellen-missy, so doraisani gave it to me.

Kamala had good reason to lie: she had filched the photograph from a few unframed ones left in the desk drawer, those not important enough to be set out in silver frames around the drawing room. Yes, the same one I mentioned earlier: Kamala carrying Elaine, Anthony on his pony, the parents on either side. Kamala quickly picked up a rather rudimentarily carved wooden horse, and asked:

- What's this you've brought?
- I made it some time ago. It will be a toy for our son.

Kamala wanted to divert Velu's attention from the photograph, which she had hidden amongst their possessions when they left Madras, not expecting Velu to see it. True, it was the only photograph Kamala would have of Elaine, but it was also the only one she would have of *Anthony*, the real reason for her haste in leaving Madras. The Smythes had no idea that Anthony, a pimply juvenile home on holiday, would lose his virginity to the comely Kamala. When his parents were at one of their many dinner parties, he had gone into Elaine's room, where Kamala slept on a mat on the floor.

But not all nocturnal visits to ayah's beds were sexual. Common enough, though perhaps not readily acknowledged, the white child found consolation in its ayah's arms. It was the accessibility of such affection, rarely available from a Victorian mother whose whalebone and binding kept maternal love out, as much as it kept her internal organs in – heart, guts, womb – inhibiting her natural feelings. In contrast, the ayah was all soft accepting flesh, yielding to the demands of a little boy or girl needing the reassurance of physical contact.

And perhaps more than just cuddling comfort was provided to infants: there are stories of ayahs giving their fretful wards sugar lumps dipped in brandy (both undoubtedly purloined; servants have always known how and when to get around locks) or little pellets of opium. No doubt some adolescent boys also lost their virginity in such familiar arms, the result of baffling urges and curiosity on his part, and yet another form of ministration on hers.

###

Was Anthony the father of this child Kamala was carrying? As soon as she knew she was pregnant, she wished she could go to a 'maruttuvacci', traditional midwife, who could abort it with herbal decoctions, aided by some physical manipulation, with crude implements if necessary. This woman's valuable services to the community went beyond delivering babies. She also rendered some postnatal care, giving the mother the right oil immediately after delivery, making her eat foods that increased breast milk and did not give the baby colic, often even giving the mother massages to bring her muscles back into shape.

Though abortion is a 'pancha-pataka', one of the five mortal sins in dharmic texts, it was practised. So was mercy killing of a deformed baby. You rarely saw a deformed or disabled child in those days: the midwife would quickly strangle it and tell the mother it was stillborn. The exhausted mother probably accepted the death without demur, even with relief. For how could people who scratched the parched unyielding fields for a living in their efforts just to subsist, sustain a useless mouth to feed, someone who needed care?

Children were inevitably a family's added labour force; a non-productive one was a burden. Boys herded skinny but voracious goats, or cows (if affordable), running after them to collect their precious dung, to be patted into cakes and dried for fuel. Girls had even heavier tasks – fetching water, collecting firewood, taking care of the babies, cleaning rice and helping in the kitchen. A male child who could bring dowry was also an economic unit, with his wife becoming another helping hand.

Far from condemning the midwife as a murderess, she was regarded as an angel of mercy, for she took on the dead baby's karma. If you take a life, you do not give the creature a chance to live out its karma, so it is added to your burden of expiable karma.

[Promila: When the belief in karma is still so widely held here, how come India continues to have this high rate of female foeticide and infanticide?
Akhil: Yeah, "what goes around, comes around", you hear that all over the world.
Advik: If so, this karmic balance-of-payments theory hasn't deterred abortionists and proponents of euthanasia.
Bhaumi: Can having a male heir atone for daughter slaughter? What's the karmic equation there?
SD: Unfortunately in India, material considerations such as dowry, override inconvenient religious tenets.]

But there was no one Kamala could turn to in this city. If the baby was born fair, the dorai *Reginald* would come under suspicion; no one would suspect a school boy capable of such outrageous precocity! Moira doraisani would turn them out immediately. It was best to leave of their own volition, with no rancour, and possibly with a few hand-outs of old clothes and toys.

Velu, of course, had no reason to doubt that he was the father and, therefore, could not understand his wife's urgency to leave Madras. Kamala managed to convince him that they had to propitiate the powerful deity in her hometown, to ensure the easy birth of their healthy son. Besides, she was only following traditional practice by having her baby in her parental home. We continue this practice, attributing it to the neonatal rest the new mother needs: she can be spoiled at home, given her favourite foods, allowed to sleep and relax, indulgences which a mother-in-law would not allow her.

Though originally there may have been a darker primitive reason: childbirth was taboo, like unclean menstrual blood, and the mother needed to be isolated. The tribe would exile the menstruating girl or delivering mother to an outhouse built specifically for the purpose. She was polluting so she could not prepare food or, god forbid, do anything auspicious like puja or going to the temple.

Another belief behind this isolation was that she could be made pregnant by the sun. Reminds me of Karna, that wonderful character, insufficiently admired, but I mustn't digress.

[Bhaumi: Was it a selfish moon not wanting her traditional opponent, the sun, casting his shadow on what was hers for but a week in the lunar cycle? But I wonder what the Moon Goddess would think of this banishment, if she is linked with menstruation, and whose rival is the sun?

SD: But in Hinduism, the moon, Chandra, is male, though in most other old belief systems the moon is female.

Sagarika: Yes, because the Moon Goddess is believed to be linked with menstruation. That word either comes from 'méhns' – moon, month – and maybe also from 'meh' (to measure), both Proto-Indo-European words referring to the moon's phases as the measure of time.

SD: Great, more words to add to my lexicon!

Bhaumi: Well, the taboo of isolation probably still exists in backward communities.

Rishab: Though I have to say it sounds like a good idea to banish menstruating women to an outhouse: they are so murderous when they have PMT!

Promila: Jee-eez, what a sexist remark!

Rishab: Sorry sorry, ladies. Oh, sorry again: it's probably not PC to even call you "ladies"!

Sagarika: And did you know that there was even a 'kōpa-āgrahārā', a room in a palace that was reserved for angry women?!

Promila: Rishab, don't even ….

Rishab: … no no, I wouldn't dare!
Fiona: But now menstruation seems to have come out of the exile-hut; the way it's flaunted, with sanitary pads regularly advertised on TV.]

###

However, leaving Madras would not solve all Kamala's problems. As her pregnancy advanced, she knew she would have to find some way of sending Velu away so that, if the baby betrayed its foreign sire, he wouldn't discover he'd been cuckolded. In his absence, she would get the midwife to strangle the boy at birth. Velu would be told the baby was stillborn and had been buried. The unsuspecting Velu had readily agreed that if "his baby" was a girl, Kamala could dedicate it to a temple; it would be good karma for him. Families who desired male progeny, or needed money, dedicated or sold their female children to temples, considering themselves blessed in their sacrifice. The custom still exists in remote pockets, though banned by law.

Fortunately, fate nudged Velu in the right direction: he had already decided to go to his village to reclaim his father's land.

~ This was such a stupid idea of yours, Kamala, to come here. Have I no pride? How long do you expect me to stay in your mother's house? People are sniggering.

~ It's only till the baby is born. In any case, we'll have to move out then. Have you thought of where we could go?

Hunh, I've been thinking of nothing else. I'm going to my village to see if I can reclaim my father's land.

###

Kamala was relieved at Velu's departure and rejoiced that they would soon have their own home. His recent tetchiness would be sweated out working his land, something he yearned for.

[Rishab: I don't get it. Why does land still have such attraction for Indians?
Advik: Yes it is extraordinary, given that little has changed for Indian farmers.
Akhil: Apart from their suicide rate going up!]

It was a mixed home-going for Velu. He was but a toddler when he left, but those who remembered his parents made him feel welcome. There was some encroachment by those who had remained in the village, but those who had returned in the hope of reclaiming their fields, banded together to re-establish their claims. Velu happily immersed himself in setting things in order. There was so much to be done.

###

Kamala was also occupied with practical matters. She had to confide in her Amma, as she did not want the services of the town midwife. Traditionally, a midwife's husband was the 'ambattan', barber-surgeon. No Indian man shaved himself and the barber was essential, also providing services like cleaning out ears, giving head massages and performing rudimentary surgery such as drawing teeth, besides being the proverbial purveyor of gossip. If there was pillow talk, no secrets could be kept between this couple. If the baby showed obvious signs of the whitewash brush, its suspect paternity would soon become common knowledge.

Kamala was young and healthy and her Amma, a veteran mother, could deal with a normal delivery. It was what they'd do with the baby after it was born that bothered Amma. If it was a girl there wouldn't be a problem, some temple could take her. But, having borne four dark daughters, the thought of killing a *male* child – his fairness the very cause of its elimination! – inveighed heavily on Amma. There was also the bad karma of taking a life.

However, the good woman did not have to grapple long with such moral issues: a distant cousin came to town and stayed with them. Mangala was a devadasi of a small village temple some distance away. Contrary to most Indian communities who value only baby boys, a male baby was a disappointment to a devadasi. Female babies were a reason for rejoicing, for girls could carry on the profession, an honourable and lucrative one when it was initiated, and in its heyday. Unlike other Indian women, devadasis even had inheritance rights and control over their own property.

[Promila: Isn't it ironic that for centuries the devadasi community cherished girls so highly, but girls are now so devalued that we are still trying to eradicate female foeticide?
SD: Well, as we shall see, a devadasi's role was also open to exploitation, even abuse. The value devadasis placed on a girl child wasn't wholly altruistic and can't be claimed as a wholly feminist triumph.
Fiona: Yes, women can and do also take advantage of and ill-treat each other.
Akhil: I guess it comes down to how much choice they actually had.]

The community's boys were only appendages, their options limited to becoming a 'nattuvanār', dance guru, or a musician, both part of the dancer's troupe. While a teacher could become rich, even earn prestige and control if he was a good enough dance guru, a musician had to dance to another's tune. Mangala's first child was a son, not only disappointing in itself, but Kumara turned out to be unfit for any of the occupational avenues open to males in their small circle. He tried to learn percussion without success, the complexities wrecked confusion in his fingers, and it was a pity he couldn't be trained as a dance teacher. He hadn't the talent or application to master classical bharathnatyam, though from an early age he loved to twirl and posture, imitating his sister Lakshmi while she practised.

When he first saw a performance of the Bhagavata Mélam, Kumara was entranced, not only by their depiction of familiar myths and legends, but that women characters – those lovely queens and goddesses – were played by men! He realised that he had an aptitude for that kind of folk dance and thenceforth, whenever any stri-vésha entertainers came to their village, Kumara would rush off to join them, donning the tinsel and brocade costumes of heroines with alacrity, and showing much flair in female roles.

What Kumara lacked in conventional talent, he made up for in affection. He was indulged by all as he was helpful, always willing to run errands, even helping his mother in the kitchen. His mischievous charm, wickedly accurate imitations and irreverent turn of speech kept the community entertained, where his musical abilities failed. When a girl was born three years after Kumara, Mangala was overjoyed and named her Lakshmi, after the goddess of prosperity. *This* child would be a devadasi, a worthy successor. Unfortunately, it gradually became apparent that Lakshmi had neither her mother's looks nor talent. But at least she would be a competent dancer, taking over from her mother, inheriting all her privileges of a devadasi.

###

However, no one could have foreseen that Lakshmi's career would be crippled* [sorry, that's a terrible pun]. It was that crisis that brought Mangala to Kamala's town, her volubility in full spate as she gushed to Amma:

- Look at my fate, sister, look at my poor Lakshmi! What can I say? It was that Kumara, naughty as ever. Lakshmi was so tired: did yoga at 5, dance practice all morning. Don't I know how tiring all those 'tatti metti adavus' are, didn't I do those steps for years? Shouldn't she have rested in the afternoon? But no, must follow her Annan to the mango grove. How many times I've told her not to eat raw fruit; it gives her a stomach ache, then how can she practise?

  Kumara was swinging on a banyan tree root and, silly girl, she always wants to do whatever her Annan does, so he lifted her up to hold a high root, and pushed her so she could swing on it. But her arms were aching with all that dance practice, and she let go. Fell right on a large stone and broke her ankle! That silly boy, shouldn't Kumara have come and called us at once? No, made her stand up and tried to make her walk. So the broken bones all got disturbed.

  Her father carried her home; she was crying in pain all the way. The ankle was smashed and look at our luck, sister, the bonesetter had gone to another village. So the barber bound it up after trying to straighten it as much as he could. When the 'kulalar' returned after three days, he reset it.

The 'kulalar', potter, was the traditional village bonesetter. When he could fashion all forms – human, animal, vessels – out of clay, who better to entrust with human flesh and bone as well? Some traditional bonesetters had spectacular results, such as the oft-quoted case of one who successfully treated Lord Elphinstone in an armitage of cane and wood, when English doctors had given up. However, handling by less skilled ones could cause a complication which resulted often enough to be given a name: "potter's gangrene".

~ A few days later, I noticed a funny smell coming from her leg, ayyō, as if the flesh's rotting. Priest told me to take her immediately to this vellakāran doctor here.

Mangala's desperation to save her daughter's foot – after all, her whole future was bound* up in it! – prompted her to seek the white man's treatment with the mission doctor in Kamala's town, before gangrene set in irrevocably.

~ The vellakāran doctor said it was good we came quickly, otherwise he would have had to cut the foot off. Ayyō imagine! Sister, don't even ask, bad things always come together. I have to take her every day for him to clean it and put medicine. I hope you don't mind us staying for some more days, sister?

~ What is this, need you even ask? You know you are welcome here.

~ Such bad luck, don't even ask. Lakshmi was initiated as a dancer only five months ago. Such a grand ceremony, we gave her such costly clothes … I had a rich landlord in mind; he would have made a good patron! Somebody's evil eye, sister.

After a few visits to the doctor, the infection had been stemmed and the foot saved, but not quite.

~ The doctor said he could try breaking the bones again and resetting the foot properly. He said her young bones will heal quickly but even so, she'll never be able to dance again. She can't put much weight on that foot, leave alone bang it in 'tattu adavu' and 'nattu adavu'.

[Well Rishab, Sanskrit not only makes use of alliteration, assonance and rhyme as mnemonics, but also to yoke opposites or pairs: karma-dharma, yoga-bhoga, Kama-Yama.]

~ Lakshmi cried so much when the doctor suggested smashing her foot. She screamed even when he manipulated it. So I thought, what is the point of breaking her leg and putting her through all that pain if she can't dance again? He has put it in this plaster and we have to come again to have it removed but I'll send Kumara back now; his father is all alone. Look at my fate, such a bad time. My Lakshmi will never dance again. So I'll have to look for another girl to take her place. Oh Kumara, you're back? What have you bought?

~ They told me these are a speciality here, Amma, and I know how much Lakshmi likes vadais.

~ Such a thoughtful boy, my Kumara.

~ Yes Mangala, our town is famous for these vadais.

Come Kumara, let's take them to Lakshmi. She's lying down inside.

Mangala's remark about having to find a girl to replace Lakshmi, gave Kamala an idea. She thought she was alone with Mangala (not realising that Kumara was eavesdropping) and took the opportunity of mentioning her problem, though she introduced it in a roundabout way:

- So Thai, you will have another baby who can take over from you?
- Ayyō, I don't want another one – and what if it's not a girl?
- So you'll look for a girl to train?
- Yes. I wanted Lakshmi to graduate quickly, start bringing some money in … but now ….
- Listen, please listen Thai, I have something to tell you. Since you need a girl to train, why don't you take my baby, if it's a girl?
- Yes, I need a replacement, but taking a baby is another matter: the training can only start when she's about four, then she'll start earning only after puberty. I was thinking of a girl already ready to train.
- Please Thai, I have a problem and it would help me if you could do this. Besides, it might be a very *fair* and beautiful girl …!
- Yenna-dee, what are you saying? What have you been up to?!
- It was when I working in that Madras house. The chinna-dorai was home from his English school. One

night, when the doraimār had gone out, I was fast asleep on a mat in missy's room when I felt someone behind me, fondling my breasts. Ayyō, I almost cried out loud in fear! He put his hand over my mouth and hissed in my ear to be quiet. I could feel his hardness against me and his heavy breathing. I kept thinking, ayyō, what if missy wakes up and sees us? I didn't want to take the risk. I wanted it to be over quickly but I soon found that he didn't know what to do.

I was also very aroused by this time, the danger itself also excited me. So I pushed him on his back and mounted him. Ayyō, he was so big! I know I can tell you all these things, Thai, you are the expert in such matters. Compared to that large bear, Velu is small. And Velu always gets on top of me; he says only that will beget a son. So, it was wonderful to be on top, controlling it, though it was all over so soon. I only had to work on him a few times, he came so quickly. I knew it was his first time. He pushed me off and left the room immediately. But oof, he had such a strong funny smell ....

~ Pah, that's all the *meat* they eat – goat, cow, pig ....

~ I thought he might come to me again. I wanted him to, so that I could pleasure him properly. If somehow we could spend a little more time without any risk of getting caught, I could make him really enjoy it, not like that quick animal coupling. But after that night, he wouldn't even look at me and would leave the room as soon as I came in.

He went back to England a few days later so I never saw him again. But I have a pōtō of him, you want to see? So fair, nice sharp nose.

- But if it is Velu's girl, won't he want to keep her?
- Velu is interested only in a boy. We already decided to give away a girl child. He doesn't even want to see it, thank god.
- We'll see. I have to bring Lakshmi back to have her plaster removed. By then you'll have delivered.

But they didn't have to wait that long, for the next day Amma and Mangala assisted in Kamala's premature but easy delivery. And yes, Velu wasn't the father. When Kamala saw her baby girl, natural emotion overcame practical contingencies as she held the plump softness against her cheek. Like Kunti who held baby Karna (he of glowing splendour), there was joy in Kamala's heart for having borne a beautiful baby – faintly burnished with a sheen foreign rather than celestial – but, like Kunti, was there sadness at having to give up an illicit child and feign a former innocence? She wished she could keep her and silently begged forgiveness for what she was going to do.

Kamala checked herself: why should she have doubts? After all, dedicating a girl to a temple was punya, justified on many grounds. Childless parents would often vow to dedicate their first child if it happened to be a girl. Or economic reasons prompted them: if the girl's family had no sons but had property, dedication ensured it stayed within the family as the girl child then became a 'son' for the family. She also earned her own livelihood as a devadasi.

A devadasi was respected, often courted, for she was 'nitya sumangali', ever auspicious. Being wedded to a divine deity, she was eternally free from the adversity of widowhood. Regarded as a bearer of good fortune, she was an especially welcome guest at weddings. Traditionally, the devadasi and her children suffered no stigma and other members of their caste received them on terms of equality. The children of a devadasi were considered legitimate and devadasis themselves were outwardly indistinguishable from married women of their own community.

Mangala also wrestled with mixed feelings; such a lovely fair baby, surely the inconvenience and cost of bringing her up would be more than worth it when she became a beautiful dancer, and the expense of raising her would be recouped when she acquired a wealthy patron? Lakshmi tried to dissuade her mother:

- There is nothing in the house ready for her. Who is going to feed her? You haven't even told Appa about this. And how will Annan feel about suddenly having another sister?

Mangala came to a compromise.

- I have to bring Lakshmi back to have the plaster removed, so I'll take the baby then but only if the Priest and my householder agree. That will also give me time to get a wet nurse and make all the arrangements.

This gave Kamala more time with the baby, time that she would rather not have had. It increased her heartache, nursing the baby at her abundant breasts. Kamala smiled at the contrast between them. The baby was fairer than the Dravidian norm and had Anthony's straight nose and cast of face. Kamala quizzically stroked the scanty hair: *this* was also a paternal feature. Indian babies were born with so much hair!

No observances were followed for this baby: not the fortnight's seclusion of the mother and her baby, nor the cradling ceremony at which a baby receives its name. This was a quiet unmarked entry for a girl whose future was uncertain, hidden.

###

Mangala and Lakshmi returned and when the plaster cast was removed, Lakshmi walked with a limp, hating this additional handicap to her already plain presence. Mangala soothed her, promising massages that would strengthen the foot. Lakshmi's tantrums were also a cry for attention; she had failed to dissuade her family from taking this baby, and her jealousy of this "sister" was thenceforth established.

Kamala was relieved and happy, knowing her beautiful baby was going to a good home. She slipped the photograph of the Smythe family into the bundle she'd prepared for the baby. Who knows, one day Mangala might tell the girl who her father was, and show her the photograph. Kamala didn't need any reminders of that phase of her life. She looked forward to starting anew in Velu's village, where no one knew her.

###

The anticipation of having a new baby in their home made Kumara a one-man reception committee. He sent for a wet nurse, decorated the house and prepared the ārathi, ritual of welcome. The baby was crying, uncomfortable with the bumpy dusty bullock cart ride. And she might also have suffered from the surreptitious pinches that became Lakshmi's habitual vents of resentment. But once the baby was wiped down and fed, she half-opened her eyes and smiled in sleepy contentment.

- Look at the eyes, Amma, so large! Yes, sweetheart, I'm your brother, your Annan. Ayyō, not much hair, Amma! But such lovely coloured skin.
- We must keep her out of the sun. No taking her off with you in the afternoons, you understand, Kumara? Must do dhristi this evening.
- What shall we name her, Amma?
- Kamakshi?
- No no, Mangala. What else but Devaki?
- Yéngō, but Devaki means black. This baby is not dark!
- So then, why do you want Devaki, Appa?
- Because I think of Devaki as "belonging to God". She will belong to God after all: dév ki.

4

After the harvest Velu went to fetch Kamala. He could talk of nothing but his village, and how happy he was to be back with his own people. He showed no interest when Kamala told him that she had a baby girl who was dedicated to a temple, though he felt disappointment – even betrayal – that his prayers had not given him the desired son. However, his faith unshaken, on their way to the village, they stopped at the Sri Angala Parameshwari temple where Velu took a vow that would guarantee a son and an easy delivery for his wife. Kamala tied a piece of her sari to the sacred neem tree in the outer courtyard, near the svyambhu anthill where the goddess is said to reside, looking like a woman in labour, her open mouth crying in pain. Under the tree there were also 'putrus', snake holes of naga-dévathas, from which the village Putlur might get its name.

That anthill image might have lingered in Kamala's mind as they approached Velu's village. From afar and the vantage point of the bullock cart, the village appeared to her like a distended anthill, mud huts seemingly growing out of a mound. Even habitation here was cyclical, in keeping with rural organic life: huts crumbled in the monsoon, returning to the earth, and yet again were resurrected out of their own decay, mud to mud, and mud from mud.

On the village boundary stood the familiar statue of Mariamma, the ascetic goddess who produces heat, her anger resulting in disasters such as drought and famine in the land, and the eruption of vesicles like small pox in humans. Grām-devatās like her were placed outside villages and were usually protective godlings. If correctly propitiated, the opposite but complimentary forces of these village deities harmonised life. They were not necessarily malevolent, though these "impure" ones were offered meat and liquor, the officiator being a shaman or witch doctor, while the "pure" godling was served by one of the sacred thread castes and offered pure food such as ghee and washed rice.

Kamala looked out for the familiar gopuram, enclosed by a red and white daubed wall, indicating a temple in use. Instead, a devil-stone stood facing east, under a sacred fig tree on which a red flag hung to mark its presence. Such stones often became the central idol of temples, with buildings growing up, over and around them.

On entering the village, tortuous paths led to its centre, an open space opposite the headman's dwelling. A magnificent peepul tree canopied the community's social hub where elders also met to take decisions. Squatting on the traditional raised stone platform, they contemplated wisps of beedi smoke like auguries. In wealthier northern villages, their problems would be passed around with the hookah – our Indian version of the old Red Indian tent-smoke, now even a phrase in American Congress.

Homes of tillers jostled haphazardly on one side, making up the bulk of this small village. Opposite, those of hereditary occupations clustered together, though represented by only one of each: barber, potter, blacksmith, astrologer-priest. Many transactions between them were still in kind. At shandi, the weekly market, or in neighbouring villages, rice, milk, vegetables and other produce were converted into currency to pay revenue, or to make purchases at fairs.

Velu had been able to reclaim his lands without much cost, so he used Perumal's savings to improve the house. Perumal's traditional mud hut had had a kitchen and only one room, which used to be curtained off for privacy. Menfolk slept on mats outside, under the walls, shrouding themselves from head to toe against mosquitoes. Kamala was delighted with Velu's additions: a new wing of two rooms and a north-facing kitchen. It was built of country bricks with thatch on wooden rafters; lower castes were allowed only bamboo poles.

Cow dung mixed with mud was smeared on the floors. Perhaps the origin of this traditional practice was to keep away evil spirits, the cow and its products being sacred. But its practical applications ensured its continuation: it kept down dust and its antiseptic properties were certainly efficacious. Besides, the floor simply absorbed the urine of a toddler; if necessary, another coating of the cow dung mixture covered the damp spot. Infants crawled around with only a leaf shaped ornament tied to their waists with black thread. No nappies were necessary and nappy rash was unheard of.

> [Bhaumi: How ecologically friendly: no water or paper wasted!
> Advik: And no pollution from detergents!]

Velu averted the evil eye by placing a painted pottery demon head on the roof. Perumal's old rooms could be used to store grain and produce, for Velu intended to increase his crops. His plans to diversify included acquiring livestock for which a shed was built at the back, instead of the lean-to where Perumal used to keep his bullock and beloved cow. Velu's ambition was to be a 'magizhan', a successful small-scale farmer, a position his father had never quite attained, and of which his mother would have been very proud.

Gourd vines sprawled over the roof and vegetables and herbs were to hand, watered by kitchen effluents. Kamala worshipped the tulasi plant every morning, in the prescribed manner. She was happy to be mistress of her own home, topping up lamps with oil, trimming wicks and lighting the lamp at sunset, a housewife's privilege.

###

Kamala adjusted to the diurnal rhythms of peasant life. Just before sunrise Velu joined other farmers setting off to their fields, to put in as much work as they could before the sun scowled too fiercely. She would go with other wives taking husbands lunch, which they ate in the merciful shade of a copse. The men would doze for a while, lulled by the soothing regularity of the industrious coppersmith birds, still at their business, tok tok tok ...

She would sometimes stay behind till Velu was ready to go home. After all, there wasn't much work for her in a house without any children. She would gaze around at the extent of tilth. Low welts of earth chequered the plain into fields, with wagtails on the ridges, snapping up gnats. She sometimes dozed off to the soporific plashing of water in the anicut, rhythmically lifted in a leather bucket from the tank by two men. After the drought, the authorities had brought more water to the area, enabling them to grow a few other commercial crops.

Slender areca nut trees wore their betel vines like shaggy coats, the thick foliage ideal for the crow pheasant to hide, during his blundering flight from tree to tree in pursuit of lizards and chameleons, or a more meagre fare of grasshoppers and cicadas. When she first heard its distinctive call she wondered how a bird managed such a booming sound, more appropriate for a large-chested monkey: hunnnf hunnnf hunnnf. She was enchanted with the many birds. Raucous as a group of sassy schoolgirls, parrots would descend on fruiting neem trees, their screeching probably giving them their onomatopoeic Tamil name: 'kilee'. Her favourite sight was the kingfisher, hovering then suddenly diving, a piece of turquoise sky plummeting into the water.

Birds were most plentiful at dusk. Babblers noisily turned over ground-leaf, hopping and squabbling in expectation of a last morsel of insects before they roosted. A large weaver bird nest, pendulous over a disused well, safe from predators, shook with so much activity that she wondered when it would collapse with the weight of its inhabitants. She enjoyed the tumbling of swallows over the tanks, gathering wet clods for their nests. When the fields were tilled, the tired soil released a zzzz of insects for exuberant drongos that swooped and lunged, snapping them up.

She loved the green of paddy fields but she knew the cost, for she had joined the women, transplanting rice seedlings, perhaps considered less backbreaking for women because of their wider hips.

###

Entertainment was pretty limited when compared to Madras, or even to her home town.

[Akhil: What choice of entertainment did they have, without electricity?
Fiona: Yes, what did villagers do after dark?
Rishab: Heh heh, hel-lo, why do you think India has such a large population?
SD: Yes, that too, but you Gen Z-s can't imagine life without your mobiles, social media, and computer games. People have always been the Indian's main source of entertainment. In joint families there was always someone to talk to.
Rishab: Yeah, but what's often desired is quite the reverse: a bit of privacy!
SD: There was also the temple, a meeting place providing secular diversions as well as divine darshan. And, given the warm evenings and the late light of summer evenings, it was easy to sit under the trees. Women also met at the well or at the tank at which they washed clothes.]

At slack periods, when they didn't have to rise early to work the fields, after the evening meal they would go to the village centre. During bright phases of the moon, young men would wrestle, sometimes dance. Kamala enjoyed dancing but they were segregated: no man to see how suggestively she could move her desirable body! Women sang while they danced, hand-clapping in a circle, or striking short coloured sticks in 'kōl-āttam'. Kamala thought of the 'pinnal kōl-āttam' that she had seen at the Kapalisvara temple festival in Mylapore. How she had marvelled at the girls who wove the ribbons into complicated plaits while they danced!

> [Sagarika: That sounds very much like the May Pole dance!]

After a day's work, they looked forward to itinerant entertainers who would beguile the evenings, a time of smoky oil lamps during which little else could be done. After the harvest and before sowing, strolling musicians and players arrived, knowing the villagers would have more to pay them, in cash or kind. And the story teller, always welcome, carrying on the oral tradition of mythological and historical information handed down to keep the heroic past alive. As he had latitude to criticise and comment on local situations, if there was a rich landlord, he was praised in the hope of a generous fee, or reviled if he was found to be stingy. This storyteller was a rung or two lower than a proper sutradhara, sometimes doubling as a schoolteacher.

Villagers had to travel for half a day or more to neighbouring villages if performing groups were visiting. Often cock and ram fights would be set up. Still a lusty wench, Kamala found it exciting to watch young men bait bulls and occasionally there were even bullock cart races. Kamala would buy all the trinkets and luxuries unavailable in their village: bangles, safety-pins, needles, ribbons, hair pins, combs. Shandi, the weekly nerve ganglia of the village, tended to offer more in the way of produce of neighbouring areas – vegetables, fruit – and they could avail of the services of itinerant cobblers and tinkers. Blacksmiths would shoe bullocks and sell ploughshares and sickles, while wheelwrights fashioned bullock cart wheels.

There was much excitement when a Ram Navami group came to the village.

- It's very auspicious, Kamala, when such groups come. They bless the village and bring good luck.
- Well, what a pity one didn't come before Perumal's famous famine ...!

Velu was struck by how his wife sounded so much like his mother at times.

###

After some months, for Kamala the novelty of village life and its surroundings was wearing off. She watched the bullock treading out the grain, interminable circles that went nowhere. It adhered to Vedic and Tantric strictures, 'dakshina mārg', going clockwise like everything auspicious: 'parikrama', the circumambulation when one entered a temple, the circles the lamp made in an ārathi ... Apparently it was in imitation of the sun's journey through heaven, of which the swastika is a representation and therefore a symbol to avert the evil eye.

The following summer was particularly relentless and the stagnation that lay heavy in the air seemed to replicate Kamala's life. She would drowse spellbound as if held down by the noonday sun, finding it difficult to rouse herself. Listlessly fanning herself with a palmyra leaf, a pregnant Kamala now viewed the landscape less charitably. Her life seemed circumscribed by those bunds that hemmed in these trifling plots of land.

A farmer living in a small village often never left it, the journey to anywhere else being hours or even days away by bullock cart. But the limited horizon wasn't just literal. He knew nothing of anything going on elsewhere – elsewhere being everything outside his village. Only itinerant bards, travelling players and priests visiting from other temples, could give them anything outside their daily experience. These peasants knew nothing beyond this world of growth and decay, unchanging no matter who the Revenue Collector was, or the vicissitudes of weather.

Did the Indian never wonder how such a small group of men ruled this country with its population, castes and sub castes, regional differences of language, customs, practices? Peasants made up the Indian majority and the villager was not interested in politics, had never thought about human rights or democracy. He was too absorbed in eking his living out of the land, shuffling the earth, his prayers furrowing equally the soil and his forehead. His main concern was how to get the water he needed and how to avoid or escape the moneylender's or landlord's clutches.

The same patriarchal trees gathered to them the farmer for his midday meal. His money was always invested in a patrimony of anicut and complicated liabilities that ground him into a trough with his seed, forever eating the produce of his fields, and seeing nothing beyond the rugged drudge of his labours that had to produce it. He saw the hand of God in everything; the Informing Spirit seemed to rise from the clods ploughed up under his feet.

So *this* is what Perumal had talked of with pain and longing, this is what he wanted for Velu? But is *this* what Velu wanted for *their son*, whose arrival Kamala awaited with increasing impatience. Velu was irked that she could even think of questioning this immutable way of life:

- Yes, Kamala, the secret of our survival is acceptance and contentment.
- Āhahā, but you still want to be a 'mazhigan'!
- There's nothing wrong with ambition that doesn't make me restless and disgruntled.
- This place doesn't even have a temple if I want to do puja for this baby I'm carrying.
- Don't worry, when I went to town to buy seed, I went to the Murugan temple and prayed for a son. But we will go to the potter to make us a figure to offer ....
- ... to offer which god? That *stone* under the peepul tree?
- Quickly spit over your shoulder. How dare you mock it? Even if it's an evil spirit in that stone, even if it is a demon, we have always propitiated it and made sacrifices to it. Let the 'kusavan' make you a figure to counter what has come out of your wicked mouth. We don't want any evil befalling us as a result of your

evil tongue.

The 'kusavan', potter, besides making pots and helping women decorate them, made figures for special circumstances: recovery from illness, women desiring offspring, animal figures for sick or stolen animals. Pujaris, special families of 'kusavans', made hollow clay horses, usually painted the colour of red earth, to set up in fields in honour of Ayanār, special deity of the caste and guardian of the fields. A renowned huntsman, Ayanār comes at night with his wives Purnā and Pushkalā, to ride these horses and drive away demons, or accept offerings and sacrifices.

Angala-amman, a grāmdevatā variation of Kali, was offered animal sacrifice in midnight pujas, to appease human inner destructive urges. As guardian of the village against ghosts and evil spirits, her shrine was set in a nearby mango grove. She was no doubt also able to scare children away from ripening fruit!

These villagers regarded "God" as being too distant and too benevolent to appease, and therefore propitiated only the village deities – divine or diabolical – to avert disasters and anything they feared: drought of the land and the womb, famine, disease, or supernatural interventions. While the Brahmin is intercessor with the high god, the sorcerer dealt with agencies of evil.

As the village did not have a priest, Velu deemed a visit to the 'valluvan' necessary. His role in the village was seer and astrologer, who performed domestic ceremonies but extended his brief to casting out devils as well. However, he was sought most often to consult the 'panchāngam', the almanac advising farmers on auspicious phases of the moon, when to sow and when to reap, when to set out on a journey, such matters mundane that required planetary sanction.

In his capacity as astrologer, however, his less enviable task was to interpret more directly the influence of celestial bodies on the personal affairs of man. This traditional wisdom of astrological slokas was contained in a stack of palm leaves held together with string [you remember sutra?] which was hung on a long nail on the wall. That made them less susceptible to termites, the same reason why anything that needed to be recorded – documents, letters, annals and wisdom – was inscribed on 'olai', dried palm leaf the width of two fingers. The stylus was anything with a sharp point: a steel pen, porcupine quill, or thorn from the acacia tree inserted under the thumbnail. (The most famous stylus is probably Ganesha's broken tusk, when Vyasa dictated the *Mahabharatha* to him). The old rounded Tamil scripts were better suited to 'olai', as angular letters would split the leaf.

Muttering as he squinted and flipped through the desiccated slats, the 'valluvan' delivered the same predictions as forecasters have done for centuries: vague declarations that could be interpreted in any light, favourable or ominous, by the anxious supplicant.

You remember the black slave, Jim, in "Huckleberry Finn"? He best sums up all attempts to predict the future, when he reads fortunes from the "huge hair ball got from the fourth stomach of an ox". Jim pronounces, with the requisite seriousness of the prognosticator:

> "We dant' know yit, what Fortune's a-gwyne to do. Sometimes she spec she'll go one way, en den agin she spec she'll go the other. De bes' way is to res' easy en let ole Fortune take her own way."

###

But at least God Murugan fulfilled Velu's prayer: Kamala did deliver a baby boy. Unfortunately, both mother and desired male offspring died in child birth. That was common enough in those days, particularly in little villages which relied on the ministrations of the village midwife with her herbal potions and unguents, ground and applied in less than sanitary conditions. The dubious aspects of her assistance also resulted in the most fatal disease of children, a form of infantile lock-jaw, caused by using a coarse blunt instrument such as a sickle, for severing the umbilical cord.

Velu bitterly regarded his fate. Alone at home, he felt the futility of such a large living space. The kitchen had been Kamala's favourite room. On a shelf she had placed the wooden horse he had carved, where it stood stiffly, regarding him with blind impartiality. Velu did not see the horse as part of the larger picture of history, as a symbol of the invader: Aryan, Muslim, British. His perspective was only personal: he remembered how fond Anthony was of his pony that he rode every morning, and Velu therefore carved that horse for him. He recalled how carelessly Anthony had discarded the toy when he had left for school, but Velu had kept it because subconsciously he equated the horse with his young master. He was also proud of his workmanship and had made it with affection.

Though Velu would have scoffed at any suggestion that he was envious of the parangi, he had subconsciously hoped to have a son who would have at least some of the white boy's advantages and privileges. Velu was not conscious of the fact that his wooden horse was a symbol of that admiration, and that he had invested it with all the promise of a son who would make him proud.

But why should he now keep this vellakāran boss' reject, when there'd be no son to play with it, leave alone fulfil all his other expectations? He hurled it with all his bitterness and anger into the fields, for termites to demolish the last vestige of his history with Kamala.

5

The pretty baby was a favourite in Mangala's household, sleeping a lot and content as long as her stomach was full. She was soon smiling her recognition of her devoted family and wet nurse. Placed on a mat on the floor, she kicked her limbs and gurgled. No musical mobiles for those babies; instead they wore tinkling bangles and silver anklets. And Devaki would fall silent in wonderment when her bangles caught the light, as her arms flailed beyond her control. Kumara, very partial to her, would often dangle a little bell or lacquered rattle over her, regaling her with baby-babble or singing songs about the stars that twinkled in the sky: "tāra maiyā, gurukula tāra maiyā ...."

Lakshmi's hostility continued, resisting all her mother's attempts at soliciting her involvement. She would not help with Devaki's bath. While Mangala massaged the baby with gingelly oil, to encourage circulation and ensure straight strong limbs, Kumara would heat the water, making sure it was the right temperature. Devaki was bathed in the manner customary for infants: the woman sat on a stone in the courtyard, or a 'mané', a slightly raised wooden platform, sari rolled up well above the knees, with her legs straight out in front of her to form a sloping ramp on which the baby was placed, face down. The baby's head was held gently between the woman's knees, so that it could breathe easily. It also prevented the water that was poured over it from getting into its nose eyes or ears, though babies still bawled in protest.

To scrub the oil off, she was rubbed with green-gram powder. A small amount of cosmetic turmeric powder was mixed in, the traditional antiseptic that would also discourage body hair. If there was dried lime peel, that would also be ground and added, to lighten the skin and for its fragrance. A lot of water was needed to ensure all the powder was washed away: it tended to get trapped in Devaki's plump folds. Oh, she was a treasure, this darling baby girl!

Mangala would then envelop her in a thin loose-weave towel, blowing into her ears, in case some water was trapped there. She would rush the baby into the room where Kumara had incense burning in a terracotta holder, a basket placed over it, to capture the incense smoke which escaped very slowly through the woven cane. Mangala would dry Devaki, holding her over the smoke; the baby would catch a cold if her hair was left wet. Kumara chuckled, as he ruffled and parted Devaki's hair, to let the heat dry the roots.

- Amma look, she's getting more hair. My oil massages are working! I must go and pick some more of that herb. Isn't she beautiful?
- Don't cast eyes, dā. Yes 'kannai', darling you're smiling, you know we are talking about you! Let's put the black spot on your cheek, keep away the evil eye.

After she was dressed in fresh clothes, Kumara loved to carry her, snuffling her soft smooth skin, with its lingering trace of incense. Lakshmi watched resentfully. Devaki was replacing her in her beloved Annan's affections. Devaki was a usurper in more ways than one; she would get the legacy that was rightfully Lakshmi's. She lost no opportunity to make the baby's life miserable, when Kumara wasn't around to protect her. Sensing her jealousy, Mangala spent as much time with Lakshmi as she could. She also persisted in trying to arouse Lakshmi's affection for the baby.

- Lakshmi, you will have to look after Devaki. I don't want her sleeping here in the kitchen, it's full of smoke. You can keep an eye on her while you sew the border on the cloth the Priest has given you.
  Where is that Kumara? I sent him to pick some greens. Now that it has rained, those greens must have sprung

up all over. They must be cooked for lunch. But he's always tarrying, talking to someone or other, that boy, so popular with everyone!

- Picking greens is not a boy's job. Why do you make him do it?
- Who else will do it? You cannot ....

Mangala almost said ... walk fast and it will take you forever. Instead, she quickly added,

- You should not go out in the hot sun.

But Lakshmi knew what her mother intended.

- I could go when the sun sets. It is so cool near the paddy fields. I hate being at home all the time. I want to be with Annan.
- You always pick flowers at dawn; you go out then, to the temple garden. And you weave such beautiful garlands. Even the Priest admires them. Punya for you 'rājāthi', my princess.

Lakshmi picked flowers and made pretty garlands for temple worship and personal adornment. Besides paddy fields, most temples had a bit of land to grow flowers needed for puja. Flowers were grown for the glory of god and for auspicious occasions. The spread of the Bhakti cult was an impetus, permitting devotion to be shown through peripheral seva such as making garlands for the temple.

Even now, if you wake up early enough, you see people picking flowers from private gardens, often carrying a hooked pole to reach into compound walls or high branches. It was sacrilegious to offer god stolen flowers so it would never occur to these devotees that they were "stealing" private property; they were only taking flowers as offerings to god, not for themselves. All flowers primarily belonged to god; what was left over could fulfil human vanity. After all, was it not god who made flowers bloom?

The Priest would leave the puja basket on the temple step for Lakshmi to fill and he would collect it later, for his early puja. It was a round shallow brass tray with a rim and a handle to which were attached two small brass deepams. It was her duty to fill them with oil and trim the wicks. In the tray she arranged flowers in circles of colour: marigolds, the orbs of intense orange ixora, the paler kanakambaram, double jasmine, magenta globes of vadamalli. She marvelled at the different subtle shades of champak: delicate or vivid orange, pale lemon or a bright yellow.

The bright pink flowers of the oleander bush added a nice colour variation. Her mother had warned her not to let the milk fall on her skin when she picked them. The milk-bush hedge that grew around the fields, to keep cattle out or in, was also dangerous. The sticky white substance it exuded could turn you blind if it touched your eyes. That is why it was such an effective measure against cattle.

After sprinkling the blooms with water, she covered them with a damp cloth so that they wouldn't go limp and brown off in the heat. One could not wash flowers, for that would dilute their sattva; for the same reason, it was forbidden to smell flowers offered to god. But as she loved the flowers' different fragrances, she would sniff her hands after she'd picked and arranged them, to see if their scent lingered. If she had handled the davana leaf, its strong scent was sure to permeate her hands.

She would fill another basket with those flowers she could thread into garlands for the idols in their puja room, or chaplets for their own hair. She loved it when her mother oiled and combed her hair and she was given first choice as to which flowers she wanted. This was a time she cherished, the touch of her mother's hands and being given her undivided attention, a time when they chatted to each other.

- 'Yenn rājāthi', my princess, such lovely thick hair! You know, when you were a child, it used to take me so long to dry your hair and you would get impatient, sitting in that closed room, wanting to go and play with your Annan.
- Yes my lovely hair: at least one thing I have that *she* doesn't!
- What a lucky man who is going to marry you, you are so talented.
- Who will marry me, Amma, when I am deformed like this?
- Nonsense, it's not a birth defect, it was an accident. In no way will you be a liability. Like the flowers you love, plants grow out of dirty soil, struggle, to give us such beautiful fragrant flowers. It's God's lesson to us:

we too, should learn to overcome life's obstacles and give of our best. And I'm going to teach you some more cooking, my famous secret recipes.

###

If the sun wasn't too hot when she finished with the flowers, Lakshmi would pick the leaves of the shikakai hedge, whose acidity made them an acceptable substitute for tamarind. If the plant had fruited, she picked the berries and dried them in the sun. They would be made into soap-nut powder to wash hair.

There was enough to keep Lakshmi occupied indoors. She swept the yard and set out chillies and spices to dry; or spread wet rice on mats, to be pounded into flour when dry. The rice flour would be made into delicious snacks. They had to be turned over to ensure even drying. After drying them in the sun, they would be stored in tins, ready to be fried as needed. Lakshmi had also to guard them from birds and chipmunks.

She hated the crows who were not only the biggest thieves, but they seemed clever enough to taunt her. They had no fear of humans and it was as if they knew exactly how far they could go. They wouldn't move if she clapped her hands or shouted "shoo shoo". Even if she made as if to get up, they would ignore her, almost as if they knew she couldn't move quickly. It was only when she was almost upon them that they deigned to hop a few steps away. She was thrilled when Kumara once shot one of them with his catapult: that kept them away for a time.

Mangala and Kumara encouraged Lakshmi's creative talents and she was gratified when praised. When she sewed clothes for the temple idols on festival days, she had an eye for giving the rich brocades even more glitter, sewing sequins all over or edging them with gold braid, the gorgeous alankara admired by worshippers.

Lakshmi was entrusted with sweeping the threshold every morning on which she drew 'kōlams', esoteric line designs [Yes, Sagarika, the same as rangōli]. The decorations also have a practical purpose. Drawn with rice flour, they feed ants who then do not venture into the house in search of food. Lakshmi would tell the 'pillayār erumbu', black ants considered sacred:

- See, I've fed you. Now keep away from our sugar!

Kōlams were also yantras to draw good vibrations to the spot, and the feet of visitors trailed this auspiciousness into the house. The Priest told her that kōlams also had religious significance:

- Some of the diagrams are abstracted natural forms, kurma matsya, Vishnu avatars. But most importantly, they are yantras, magical shapes, their intertwined lines form nets to catch god's favours.

A mantra is interwoven into a yantra, the aural and visual reinforce one another. Just as a mantra has to have a precise and correct measure of syllables, its yantra is a unique linear design and together they function as a prayer for a specific outcome. So, while the mantra is chanted, the yantra is the web to entrap 'karma-phala', a particular result prayed for [preyed* for, ha! Don't you get it? Like the spider's web catches its prey!]. Yantras catch god's favours streaming from the firmament, vibrations from heaven.

Is that so improbable? What is a TV antenna then, if not a terrestrial metal yantra to draw desired waves from the satellites man has thrown up there? The dish has to be in the right location, facing the correct way, to attract desired wavelengths, just as a yantra has to be correct in form and position to catch divine benedictions. Wherever people live now, you almost certainly see dish antennae, like so many baby birds with their beaks open, waiting for the mother bird to feed them, not with food, but with entertainment, sustenance of modern man.

And with that pernicious spread of time-pass has come the gradual diminishing of that amazing Indian impetus to beautify the everyday, far beyond the expedient demands of their temporal nature: rangoli, kathakali masks, Yakshagana head-gear, Madhubani paintings on walls, down to the lovingly wiped fruit and vegetables artistically arranged in a market stall. Even baby walkers were decorated with bells and colourful bands of lacquer.

Talking of mobility: our rajas had elaborate caparisons, howdahs and livery for their elephants, camels and horses. The more humble have always adorned their livestock, because caring for animals included beautifying them. And there's an interesting carry-over of this impulse to decorate our means of transport. We see lorries, buses and autorickshaws painted and decorated, much as the owners' forebears would have decorated their bullock carts and tongas.

> [Akhil: So why are our cars not similarly decorated?
> SD: I think the car is a sort of missing link in the evolution of Indian transport. The motor car was introduced by the white man and was regarded as a mark of sophistication and progress. For the Indian who could afford it, possession of this status symbol was emulation of those western attributes. He wasn't going to besmirch it with gaudy native embellishment! Whereas motorised public transport graduated directly from animal-drawn vehicles and was not associated with classy style, as bullock cart and tonga owners retained that 'naïf' impulse to decorate their vehicles.]

Temporality has always been a keystone of parampara, as if to underline Indian philosophy's notion of the passing of all things, the permanence of none. The willingness to expend time and loving attention on such daily creations that are obliterated as regularly, might well be the reason why Indian creative impulse and artistic traditions have been kept alive. Today's lack of time and the erosion of religious impetus and significance, suggests an inevitable waning of such cultural heritage.

###

Till Devaki's dancing lessons began when she was four, it was an enchanted childhood, pampered by her adopted family and adored by the village. Only Lakshmi's resentment grew apace. Kumara had been *her* constant companion, always amusing. But now, in his eagerness to show Devaki the places he loved, he was inadvertently inconsiderate of Lakshmi's handicap. He would run on ahead, with Devaki not far behind. There seemed so little time, so much to explore and do. Kumara would briefly slow down when Lakshmi protested, dragging her leg along as best she could, her bitterness not lagging far behind.

Though Mangala tried to get Devaki to rest in the afternoon, the children were not deterred by the heat, Kumara leading the way to indulge in simple pleasures, unaware that Lakshmi couldn't join in when they swung on banyan roots that hung like shaggy beards. She slipped in the mud when launching the boats Kumara made from dried seed pods of the silk cotton tree, after they had burst and released their white fluff, which the children chased.

Wealthy households that had luxuries like mattresses and pillows, harvested and stored the pods before such natural wasteful profligacy, and awaited the annual visit of the cotton cleaner, his strange tool making a distinctive twanging sound. This was suspended from a beam and the string struck with a dumb-bell shaped implement, the vibrating string fluffing the cotton, ready to be filled into bedding. Mangala had told Devaki of a big carved wooden bed with a soft mattress and pillows bought from

Madras, that she'd seen in her patron's house. Devaki could only dream of such luxuries, for they only slept on mats on the floor and wooden blocks served as pillows, with a dip carved in the centre to accommodate the head, a poor rustic version of the beautifully decorated porcelain Chinese "princess pillow".

Mango trees made natural climbing frames from which Kumara and Devaki would swing upside down. At fruiting time, when the trees were pendulous with golden fruit, they had to compete with raiding troops of monkeys, or watch out for the vicious large fire ants that formed formidable lines, jealously patrolling the mangoes' oozing sap with military zeal. Kumara teased them by placing twigs in their path, to see their puzzled gesticulation.

- Annan, stop it. Poor things, they are throwing up their hands in surrender, saying "What can we do with this naughty boy? What antics will he think of next?"

Devaki avoided the huge banyan tree, where a wizened woman sat, her lips parched with mouthing her silent pleas, counting them off on her mala, bead by bead. Not only did she look like the witch of the stories children heard, but nearby there were snake stones, commonly seen under sacred trees.

- Isn't she scared of snakes? I believe they come wherever there are these snake stones.
- Snakes come at nāga panchami to drink milk that is offered to them. They won't bother a poor old woman like her.

It was only when Kumara said he would go with her that Devaki agreed to approach the woman. Repetitive syndrome had curled her fingers so that the other hand had to prise them open, when she accepted the banana from Devaki, who stayed a cautious arm's length away.

- Ayyō Annan, did you see? Those fat mala rudraksha beads were almost smooth. How many times must she have rubbed them?
- Yes, poor thing, she's just waiting for death. When her family left the village, she felt she wouldn't survive the journey so she stayed on, believing the Lord would look after her. See, she wasn't scary, was she, poor thing.
- I'm going to bring her some food every day.
- It will have to be only fruit or maybe watery buttermilk. I don't think she can digest anything else.

###

The energetic and enterprising Kumara was always on the lookout for something novel and his roaming made him a good source of information for the community. Dommara troupes would sometimes visit larger fairs. This nomadic tribe was famous for its acrobatic feats, tumbling, juggling, tight-tope walking, pole dancing ....

> [SD: I see the gleam in your eye, Rishab, you young buck, but no, this is nothing like the pole dancing you are thinking of.]

- Oh Devaki, you should have seen that pole he was balancing on: it was higher than a coconut tree!
- It must have been two poles tied together, Annan, because how can you get one pole that is so long?
- You're right Lakshmi. Anyway, and then, when he was standing on top of that tall tall pole, can you imagine, he also balanced five pots on his head!
- And where are the things I asked you to buy, Kumara?
- Oh Amma, I gave the acrobat some money because I have never seen anyone doing something so dangerous.

Before she could scold him, he added endearingly:

- But see, Amma, I bought you a comb. Their women were selling so many kinds, and I know you complain when the girls get lice in their hair and you would want a nit-removing comb.

###

It was Kumara who announced that a festival was being held in a neighbouring village, with a performance of wooden puppets. Kumara went on ahead to make sure they got the best viewing places in the yard next to the temple. The others came later, with food Mangala had made, and some provisions and cooking utensils, as it was a three day affair. A stage was erected surrounded by lamps, while the audience sat in the open or under crude temporary cover. As the news spread, people from neighbouring villages congregated, arriving before it got dark, as the performance started at nine at night and would end before dawn.

In big towns, the festival was celebrated by larger groups for forty days. This was a scaled-down version so had only a 'vidhushak', a downgraded sutradhara. He's more like a clown and usually the sutradhāra's sidekick. [Not my league!]. It was, of course, an all-male cast and Kumara thought that the young man playing Draupadi should have been far more beautiful; he had no grace. Now, if only *he* had been in that role ... ! Devaki dozed off in Mangala's lap, after her initial enchantment with the fantastic wooden figures and bright painted masks waned, and after songs and jokes, when the action ground down to more philosophical narrative.

She was woken by Kumara, who was already up cooking uppuma for breakfast.

- Come on, come on, you can't be so lazy.
- Ayyō Annan, couldn't you have let me sleep a little longer?
- Ok tomorrow I won't wake you. But I heard that today a group of acrobats has come and they are going to do hook swinging! We have to see that, so eat up. Amma, I believe they swing high up in the air, holding on to the hooks with only their teeth!
- Silly boy, you are scaring her! No, rājāthi, don't worry, they don't fall.
- After that, we can go and see how the Dommara boys do some spinning tricks. I believe they use a string

with two sticks, and they throw something high in the air and catch it on the string, without even looking!

[SD: Yes you're right Sagarika, it's the same as diabolo, juggling an hour-glass-shaped piece of wood on a string attached to two batons. Apparently it originated in China and was taken to the west by a Frenchman. Dommaras are like gypsies, so they must have picked up this skill during their wanderings. Some say that their name connects them to the Dōms of north India.]

After the third night, the play ended as the sun was just rising, with a hymn to the sun god. Kumara reluctantly helped pack, sorry to see the group go. He was not looking forward to the bone-punishing bullock cart ride home; strange how he didn't feel it when going to any entertainment. Carts made of bamboo and wood were assembled with hemp or coconut fibre rope, so had enough give in every joint to withstand the rough roads, or more usually the track ruts they traversed. The catamaran, too, braved rough seas for the same reason: 'katta-maram', Tamil for "wood tied together".

6

Devaki was soon old enough to start dancing lessons. Dedication rituals had to be performed before puberty, before a girl turned "unclean". Menses was "heating" according to traditional classifications – along with blood, passion, sex and even certain foods and spices – and it was thought expedient to keep such dangerous phases under control.

A nattuvanār had to be found, for after Lakshmi's accident, her dance teacher had left. Mangala sent word to the famous temple in Thanjavur, the large town in which she grew up. She had been sold as a child to the devadasi family and the 'thai-kizhavi' – the beautiful Sundari – adopted her officially. A thai-kizhavi was a retired devadasi, staying on in the house allotted her by the temple as a sort of den mother, in charge of her current protégés. Under Hindu law administered in British courts, devadasis were the only class of women who were allowed to adopt girls to themselves. Adoption was otherwise a male preserve and they could adopt only males.

> [Promila: I am amazed at how liberated Indian matriarchal societies were, precursors of modern-day feminists.
> SD: As we learn more about Devaki's life, I think you'll find it's not as clear-cut as that.]

Thanjavur was not only a great centre of music and dance, poetry and drama, but an unusual amalgam where an entirely different Indian community existed comfortably with the original inhabitants. Maratha rulers absorbed all that was best in the Tamil area they conquered. It was symbiotically enriching, with the injection of Kshatriya power and money into Brahmin learning and culture. The existing body politic was also fattened with rich lardoons of Tamil, Telugu and Marathi vernaculars.

There was an infusion of north Indian music and dance, and even that of the foreign rulers. The court's orchestra could play waltzes to entertain foreign guests, and "God Save the King" was a staple of the brass band's repertoire. The famous Tanjore Quartet thrived under the Maratha court's patronage. There were infusions of Telugu poetry to which the famous dance gurus could choreograph new padams and 'svarijathis'. When the kingdom was pocketed into the Madras Presidency, culture seeped out, with the Tanjore Quartet's descendants and students seeking patronage at other courts and temples.

Thanjavur's huge religious and artistic culture was Mangala's rich inheritance. Her foster mother, Sundari, was not only a good dancer and great beauty, she had been taught by the best, as her teacher came from the respected lineage of Vazhuvoor nattuvanārs. In turn, Sundari's mother, Padmavathi, also boasted a proud heritage, linked to the Tanjore Quartet.

Padmavathi's guru was too old to teach Sundari, but would shake his head in regret when he saw her superb abhinaya, saying Sundari was fit to entertain the Tanjore court in its heyday, and would have been covered in pearls by the raja. Sundari's guru was well-versed in the Natya Shastra, passing on his knowledge and experience to his pupils.

She grew up with Shankara, a musician in the temple's 'péria-mélam'. Only major temples had these large bands. Both Mangala and Shankara absorbed culture from the nattuvanār, and religious philosophy from the very learned temple priest. Shankara was as quiet as Mangala was lively, her impulsive garrulousness bubbling over uncontained. He accompanied her to her posts in various temples and, as she was wedded to God, he was only her unofficial "husband", though where the law could not cement their relationship, their abiding affection did. Like all good Indian wives she never used his name, calling him "father of ...", or referred to him in the third person and respectfully addressed him only as "thou". Kumara and Lakshmi regarded Shankara as their father. Genetic verification was not generally sought in that community, where a patron could have fathered a devadasi's child, though sometimes attempts were made to foist paternity onto him.

> [Sagarika: So an early #metoo movement?
> SD: Trying to pin paternity on men for financial gain has probably always existed, though, to devadasis' credit, few seem to have exercised that option, as they were not only comparatively financial independent, they also valued their lives free of such male control.]

In India under various rulers, the devadasi community studied and kept alive its dance and music, enabling our generation to appreciate and avail of that precious inheritance. There was no other access to these arts except from this singular stronghold of oral tradition, which could be imparted only in practice, rather than by theory or book learning. Mercifully beyond any Macaulayan inroads, verbal teaching and practical instruction continued, the more important as dance and music were not notated. While daughters of temple women became dancers, sons continued as dance teachers, musicians or temple staff.

At the nattuvanār's dance hall boys were taught from childhood, the training to be a teacher even more taxing than that of the dancer. Their véshtis bound with a sash and bells on their feet, the boys went through all the exercises geared to mastering the repertoire of the dancer. Once he was a fully-fledged guru, he had then to impart all this knowledge to a devadasi. The novitiate also had to gain proficiency in classical music, reciting the 'jati' syllables and beating the tālam with cymbals, sometimes on the mridangam, the south Indian drum. He studied Tamil, Telugu and Kannada to interpret the text, understand its concealed meaning, and to bring out the best interpretation of a padam, a dance set to a love poem. Sanskrit was optional but desirable, as he often sang hymns as part of the sixteen rituals in temple services.

Living as part of the temple establishment, he absorbed its milieu directly and intimately. Many temple rituals were later adapted for stage performances. Most temple walls were decorated with religious or legendary figures and often depictions of myths, that provided inspiration for light fleeting emotions visually transmuted into dance, resulting in first-hand creativity. Living alongside rich musical traditions, dance gurus heard the best music of their day, which inspired creative choreography.

Their shared inheritance and way of life meant a seamless conveyance of all the characteristic knowledge, culture and racial wisdom from guru to disciple, though senior gurus would not share the tradition with the unworthy, ever vigilant to preserve its purity.

The arrival of colonists changed the rules of patronage, their new dispensations bringing an element of shame to this class of women. Initially royalty was affected, which in turn affected the fortunes of local landowners who supported temples. Over a period of time, the very climate for indigenous arts changed. Nineteenth century British evangelical attitudes effectively blocked any widespread study of Indian art and culture, with Hinduism being particularly repellent. Traditionally there was no shame associated with this class of women, but fanaticism – mostly of missionaries and moralistic Victorian memsahibs – condemned 'sadir', reborn as bharatanatyam, as immoral and bawdy. They equated "nautch" with fallen women and heaped shame and opprobrium on devadasis.

This approach infected some westernised Indians who, if they didn't actively denounce the "shameful practice", came to look down on it, consequently denying education to Indian girls: only "those women" were educated, studying languages, poetry, music and goodness knows what else …! Respectable girls learned only to be good wives, mothers and housekeepers. Domestic economy was best learned at home. What need of schools? Education had to have a functional end and utility.

That was often applicable to boys who followed in their fathers' trades, keeping shop, tilling the land, or artisans remaining in guilds. Professions are still largely family preserves, whether in Bollywood or corporate houses. The term "house" itself is a giveaway, denoting a cosy enclosure, the privilege of a chosen few.

> [Fiona: So why is dynastic succession in politics slammed? After all, it conforms to that traditional pattern: royalty appointed their heirs to the throne, so politicians are now doing what rulers always did.
> Akhil: Come on, that argument doesn't hold good in a democracy!]

It was only later, with the rise of an Indian westernised educated middle class, that a girl's education gradually ceased to be looked at askance. In fact, with characteristic Indian entrepreneurship, "Degree" soon became a marketable marriage bazaar tag, and not just for girls. As for "Foreign Returned", that is a qualification parents do not fail to mention when advertising their children as desirable spouses. [So you lot are in great demand!].

This attitude shift also saw devadasi sadir achieving honoured status as bharathnatyam, one of India's leading performing arts, but the dubious reputation of the devadasi lingered. I remember my sister – she couldn't have been more than six years old – being ticked off by my grandmother for standing with her hands on her hips, because that was a dancer's basic position. My grandmother didn't want any girl in her family being mistaken for one of *those*: "Shameless girl, posing like a devadasi; take your hands down at once!"

The revivalists who wanted to preserve the traditional form of sadir dance were mostly from Brahmindominated Theosophical circles. Some tried to counter the approbation of Christian orthodoxy with Hindu amelioration, claiming it was a form of natya yoga that enhanced an individual's spiritual plane. Not a wholly unjustified assertion, as spiritual dimension was an integral part of a devadasi's original purpose.

Most teachers continued to be men, as devadasis were still regarded as morally undesirable, unfit to teach impressionable girls from respectable society. As upper castes started learning these arts, the devadasi fell between two schools: she could no longer dance in temples, nor was she wanted as a dance teacher. Her means of subsistence taken away, she perforce turned to prostitution. In an about turn, women have now reclaimed dominance in dance performance, teaching and choreography.

###

Mangala had already adopted Devaki, who was considered her own daughter, so no formal application needed to be made to the Chief Revenue Officer of the Division for orders to dedicate her. She made an application to the temple authorities, so that Devaki could be heir to Mangala's family and temple service. When sanction was granted, the Priest appointed the auspicious day and time for the initiation ceremony: 'pottu-kattu' or mangalsutra-tying wedded her to the deity, as Brahminical tradition views marriage as the only religious initiation permissible to women. The Priest executed the document and the dedication ceremony was performed in the temple. Temple funds covered expenses for this rite of passage.

On the day of her 'sādhaka puja', initiation to her dance profession, there was rising earlier than usual in the household. Mangala supervised Devaki's bath, reciting the right mantras with each potful of water. Devaki loved the special smell of the new clothes she put on. Kumara was major domo, making ready everything for the initiation to begin Devaki's dance training, similar to the ritual of the first readings of a Hindu boy being dedicated to his guru.

While Devaki dressed, Kumara picked kusha grass whose tenacious roots overcome the harshest soil, so that it is offered particularly to Ganesha, proverbial remover of obstacles.

> [Advik: No wonder kusha grass is widely used in our pujas. It's said to absorb 60% radiation and has healing properties.]

- Lakshmi, Amma wants you to make a garland of these. We are taking Devaki to the Ganesha 'kōil' to propitiate him.
- All I hear is Devaki Devaki Devaki! You stopped loving me from the moment she came. Why should I do anything for her? What does she do for me?

But, as usual, Kumara prevailed. He persuaded her to mould an image of Ganesha out of turmeric paste and thread a 'malar mālai' of flowers for Devaki to wear in her oiled plaited hair. In spite of herself, Lakshmi found herself caught up in the excitement of Devaki's ceremony.

The acknowledged authority on decoration, Lakshmi got Kumara to pick fresh mango leaves which she separated, wiped each leaf with a damp cloth and laboriously folded the tip over a string, fastening it with a bit of broomstick. When the string was full, the frill of pointed leaves – a 'thōranam' – was fixed over the lintel of the door, in auspicious welcome. She made garlands to decorate the living room of the house. Paddy husk, a symbol of abundance, was spread on the floor. The paddy was donated by the temple, for even this small temple had enough land to cultivate it for their needs.

The guru sat on a 'mané'. Standing in front of him, Devaki grasped the middle of a twisted sari, held on either end by Lakshmi and Kumara, one reluctant, the other ever eager to be part of the proceedings. The nattuvanār held her ankles and moved her feet in the first simple steps: théyy-yā, théyy-yee, théyy-yā, théyy-yee ...

###

Thereafter, it was a long and arduous training that usually took seven years. Whether or not she had a talent for dancing, it was a routine from which there was no break, no matter how tired she was, no matter what her personal feelings were.

> [SD: See Promila, this is why I cautioned you about putting too feminist an angle on a devadasi's way of life. Ultimately, it's all about choice: what realities hedge one's options.]

Lessons started early at 5.30 though it was only some yoga and musical training, mostly vocals. At 6.30, the Guru took a break till 8, giving everyone time for breakfast. The rest of the morning was governed by the 'thattu kazhi', a stout short stick that beat out its relentless measure on a block of wood, as if earthing the dance. Without bells (for those could be worn only by fully-fledged dancers) Devaki's feet performed preliminary 'adavus', set patterns of steps. The gruelling training finished at midday, time for lunch and the customary post-prandial rest. If Devaki wasn't too tired, the children would play a board game with tamarind seeds, or knuckle bones with cowrie shells. At the cool evening hour of six, classes were resumed, though by lamplight only the far less taxing abhinaya and mudra could be taught, to bring the day to an end at eight, in time for dinner.

Devaki had no energy for the energetic expeditions she once enjoyed with Kumara, though he tried to be part of her training as far as he could – and at least on one occasion in a way she least expected:

- What are you doing here? Why are you wearing my clothes and jewellery? Ayyō, you've even used eyeliner and lip colour ....

Kumara did an elegant twirl.

– You still don't get it, do you? Let's just say I'm rehearsing because I want to take part in the stri-vésham, where all the roles are played by men. I want the part of the beautiful apsara, Rambha. I wish I could join one of those troupes. They travel all over. One group told me about this temple where they take boys like me to serve in the temple, instead of girls like you. And they also take 'pottans' – you know, those who are born without anything definite down there. Oh don't look so shocked.

Pah, there was no rejoicing when I was born. A boy can't be dedicated to a temple; he's only a devadasi's camp follower. I wasn't going to be in a 'chinna-mélam' as a minor musician, having to dance to a dancer's tune – not even if *you're* the dancer, my rājāthi.

And I've heard stories about how our gods change, how there's even a form of Shiva as half-man half-woman, imagine that! So I'm not doing anything so wrong. If our gods can change sex whenever they like, why can't I?

But keep a watch out for Amma, while I get changed. If she sees me like this, I've had it. Āhahā, why are you turning away so coyly? Don't worry, my poor innocent darling, you're going to see plenty of *this* in future, when you get a patron!

###

True, Mangala hadn't a clue about Kumara's orientation. His feminine looks and mannerisms put him in a sexual limbo, but those in the community tacitly acknowledged it. Behind his back they called him 'ponna-sāmi' (girl-man) or pottan, for which I've coined a new word, 'nonorchid'.

> [Bhaumi: What do flowers have to do with it? Orchids happen to be my favourite.
> SD: Ah, you're in for a shock: orchid comes from the Greek word for testicle!
> Rishab: Ha ha ha, so if I give a girl a bunch of orchids, the real message is "it's all balls"? Ha ha ha hilarious!
> SD: Hitler was famous for being a monorchid, a one-ball man. The word I've invented – 'nonorchid' – in this case means no-balls-at-all. So pottan implied that Kumara had no lust in him, no sexual drive in any direction.]

The issue came up only when Mangala mentioned marriage to Shankara. Lakshmi's foot had healed and her limp was only slightly perceptible so Mangala was looking for a suitable husband for her. She'd amassed enough wealth to make the dowry tempting.

- Yén-gō, isn't it time we also looked for a daughter-in-law with a good dowry, to offset the big one we'll have to give for Lakshmi? Such an affectionate boy, our Kumara; everyone likes him. I've already told go-betweens to find a boy for Lakshmi; they can also find Kumara a girl at the same time, no?

~ Leave it, Mangala. Kumara being what he is, why should we make some girl's life a misery, though many boys like him get married. What to do? It's our fate. As you say, he is so loveable, so whatever he is or isn't, love him is all we can do. And don't we even accept our Lord Shiva himself, as Ardhanareeshvara ...?

~ Ay-ay-yō, yénnān-gō, what, what are you saying ...?

The upset Mangala rushed to Guruggal, as they called their Priest. Could he ratify religious precedence for people like Kumara?

~ Why are you crying woman, when it is even sanctioned in our shastras? The body is just jiv-atma, a vehicle of the spirit to carry us to God, to unite us with param-atma. So we have to accept anybody's svabhāv, one's intrinsic nature, except deviancies that harm others.

When philosophy didn't stop her tears, he tried to tease her out of them:

~ Why are you worried? He has all the 'lakshanās' – auspicious attributes – of a girl, not a very beautiful one, but they might appeal to some men ....

~ Chee chee, yennā Guruggal, what are you saying?

~ Listen, you might as well admit what your husband has had the wisdom to perceive and to accept. And you know why he is wise? Because he knows, as I do, Kumara is a woman in his looks and movements not only when he is in stri-vésham on stage, but in life he *thinks* and *feels* like a woman ....

- Ay-ayyō, *my* Kumara?!
- Why do you think he went to Koovagam during Chittarai? Oh, you think he went there because it's some ordinary 'kōil'? It's a temple for eunuchs. Don't you know that story? In the *Mahabharatha*, Aravan was Arjuna's son, a brave warrior who agreed to be 'kalappali', a human sacrifice on the battlefield, to ensure victory for their side. But dead bachelors couldn't be cremated, they were only buried without proper funeral offerings. No one would marry that poor sod Aravan, because no woman wanted to become a widow. So Krishna took pity on him and took a female form and married him just for a night, as the next morning he would die. To celebrate that wedding anniversary, eunuchs dress as women and "marry" at that temple.

  Face the facts, woman ... Come come, don't worry, there are so many instances in our Puranas where characters have crossed over, sometimes so many times – Ila, Shashin, Amba, Riksharaja – so that I forget what sex they are. Yes, it's quite a list, even I can't remember all of them.

There you are: yet another example of our gods anticipating what we might do, so that there are few practices we humans indulge in that are not sanctioned by divine example.

- No, the important thing is what such a person *perceives* as his or her nature. Even our myths stress that fact. Some of them just took on the body of the opposite sex because of a curse or boon, you know our stories are full of such fantastic nonsense.
- But I'm worried about his future: if he doesn't get married, who will take care of him when we are gone?
- I suppose Devaki will be around for as long as he is. Why does he need a wife? I believe he loves to cook. And he will in some way always be attached to this temple.

Those who adopt the roles and many practices of the opposite sex are now called 'supernumerary gender', but centuries ago Hindu philosophy had a category for them: 'tritiya-prākriti', third nature, which they describe as an inborn nature that combines both male and female properties. Homosexuals and transgenders were recognised for their unique nature and incorporated into Vedic belief. They were not punished or persecuted under ancient Hindu law, and elaborate descriptions of homosexuality can be found in the Kamashastra.

Homosexual men are referred to in Sanskrit by several different names including napumsaka, shandha and kliba. These words are often mistranslated into English as "eunuch" but they actually refer to a wide range of men who are impotent with women for various reasons. Such men formed a distinct social class in ancient India and were considered to be sexually neutral by nature. The

Sanskrit names for lesbians are svairini or nastriya and were similarly impotent with men.

LGBTs MTFs FTMs et al are not uncommon in mythology. In some cases, oscillating between ambiguities was to practise deception: Arjuna in exile, Thor, Odin. They usually needed gods as gender-lenders, who would curse them (Tiresias) or grant boons (Shikhandi). No trips to Thailand in those days!

Hinduism considers universal creation as unlimitedly diverse, so the recognition of a third sex is simply one more aspect of this comprehensiveness. Gender-ambiguous persons were traditionally awarded a semi-divine status and their participation in religious ceremonies, especially as cross-dressing temple dancers, was considered auspicious: a symbol of good luck, peace and cultural prosperity. That is why hijras are welcomed at weddings and auspicious occasions, because some still believe that people of the third sex have special powers that allow them to bless or curse others.

It's a pity then, that today some people who stringently reassert our "cultural heritage" are so selective: the official and non-official groups and individuals set themselves up as gatekeepers of society's standard boundaries, persecuting those "others" – LGBTs MTFs FTMs et al – though, as with everything in India, if one pays a ferry man, one can cross over.

Since moral-policing also rejects "decadent western culture", it condemns girls for dressing "provocatively" and behaving "loosely". To be consistent, they would also have to smash the carvings on almost all our old temples – those bastions of our religion, heritage and culture – of full-breasted females in diaphanous garb that is certainly more revealing than any outfits girls wear today. And rewrite Hindu myths about our many "immoral" women.

One finds gender-blenders in other societies as well: the Spanish encountered native American 'berdaches' who had a special role in religious ceremonies; both sexes participated in the transvestite celebration of the Aphroditus' cult; the very first geishas who entertained customers were men. Many regions in India sanction cross-dressing: gotipua dancers in Orissa, some Krishna cults where men worship him as gopis … Chaitanya, for example, donned women's clothes to be a Radha for his beloved Krishna. Certain tantric sects in Bengal believe that dressing like the opposite sex makes for understanding and identifying with it, so that they can achieve complementary perfection within themselves.

> [Bhaumi: Anthropology endorses this. In some cults, cross-dressers and eunuchs wear women's clothes to generate shakti within themselves, and shamans also wore women's clothes and ritual ornaments for the same reason.
> Promila: But can't it also be a form of 'dvésha', aversion, wherein man imitates woman so that he can *master* the thing he fears? He tries to supersede her by imitating her?
> Fiona: Could all this recent sadistic crime against

women derive from man's hateful *envy* of woman's ability to be a reproductive force? Primitive man worshipped Mother Nature for her generative powers; because woman can procreate, she seems to have some magical communion with nature that the male doesn't?

Bhaumi: Yes, that could explain it. So many men feel they have no control over their lives in today's society; they feel frustrated, impotent. Rape is an easy way of reasserting their power.

Promila: And because sex is an urge over which man has least control, in a sense, he fears it, fears the way it can take hold of him and make him do irrational things. As woman is usually, "normally", the one who arouses this instinct of lust, he projects this fear/dread onto her and therefore seeks to control her, rather than try to control his own instinct. He puts her in purdah, to shield his own lust. He puts all kinds of restrictions on her, as if that would absolve him of his responsibility in the problem.

Bhaumi: Yes, it is all about control: he can only control her by dominating her and keeping her subservient, in the hope that that will mitigate his own lack of control.]

###

Mangala was also thinking of Devaki's future. She

was growing tall, rather too much so. She wondered if Devaki would be a trifle too tall as a dancer when she finally graduated to dance in the temple. The Natya Shashtra stipulated 'lakshanās', desirable specifications, for the ideal dancer. Besides the dilution of dark skin, her height was another feature which betrayed her foreign paternity, though those unusual aspects could work in her favour when seeking a patron.

But no use speculating, for Mangala sometimes had serious doubts if Devaki would overcome her stubbornness; she was almost revolting against her dance training. She hoped Kumara hadn't put any silly ideas into her head; she must have a word with him. What did the girl think she could do, if not be a devadasi? And it would soon be time for her 'sadanku', coming of age ceremony. Her breasts were budding, surely her first menses was imminent.

Now Lakshmi could exult, seeing Devaki's tears, her rebellion against the steps she had relentlessly to repeat till she got them right. She was a reluctant pupil at best, her tender body finding the training strenuous in the extreme. Mangala gradually hardened the soles of her feet, making her go barefoot most of the time. Her body ached, though Mangala massaged her with herbal oils, to relieve muscle pain as much as to keep her limbs straight and strong.

Devaki loved her massages when she sensed that the hands conveyed caring. She could also perceive moods and feelings: she sensed when her mother was relaxed and her hands communicated tenderness, but if Mangala was edgy with thinking of all the undone tasks, she could sense impatience in her fingertips. When Lakshmi once grudgingly obliged her mother by massaging Devaki's back, the indifferent hands bore no soothing, no stroking palms imparting warmth.

On one occasion when Kumara oiled Devaki's hair, he showed her all the moves the new barber had worked on his head:

- This is like a monkey looking for lice. Here's a hen pecking for grain. And this is like playing the tabla, taka-dum taka-dum, dum-taka-dum.

But she enjoyed most of all the gentleness she felt through his fingertips when he slowly massaged her head with circular movements, loosening the scalp to encourage circulation.

###

Devaki chafed at the life of ease Lakshmi led:

- Lakshmi has always hated me, Annan, though I've always tried to be nice to her. She was so mean to me when I was very young. I can't understand it, even now she's always teasing, tormenting me in little ways. I don't like to complain to Amma. Or Appa. I love him so much but I don't know how he feels about me.
- He's always been undemonstrative and quiet. Not like Amma, who's the opposite. He never picked us up as

babies and we've had very little physical contact. But I did see him stroking your cheek and cooing over you as a baby, when he thought no one was looking. He adores you but he's never going to show it, so don't expect it.

Yes, of course Amma puts Lakshmi before you in her affections but that's because she feels bad about her misfortune. She's always had ambivalent feelings about Lakshmi not being a beauty, being so ordinary. And Lakshmi has failed as a devadasi's daughter. Poor Amma was thrilled when Lakshmi was born: a daughter who could inherit her position! But Lakshmi hasn't got any of the talent or attributes a dancer needs, so thank goodness Fate has made sure she can't dance. So after the accident Amma feels she must make it up to Lakshmi, now that she can't be her successor. Knowing that, Amma has been shrewd enough to accumulate enough to ensure a big dowry so that Lakshmi can be married off to some musician or peasant.

Peasant? If you mean literally, so what if his plot of land is no bigger than the temple's? As long as a wife is free of this *slavery*. Annan, I *hate* what I have to do! Wish I could get married and just be looking after the house, children...

You think *you* are enslaved?! Wives are the worst kind of slaves: they don't even get paid for all the work they do. You'll never have a mother-in-law, so you'll never know what being a slave means! You can continue to live in this house, enjoy the rice grown on the land, inherit your property and pass it on to your daughter … other women would envy *you*! Of course Lakshmi resents that she's had to give up all that for you. But she's also jealous not only because you are prettier, but because you are fairer. Skin colour is one thing no one can change, no matter how much effort they are willing to put into it!

[Fiona: Amen to that! So it's shocking that cosmetic companies are still allowed to promise "fair and lovely" skin! Just aint gonna happen!]

7

Mangala instructed Devaki in knowledge and art of another kind, no less indispensable to a devadasi, 'ars amor'. It was very business-like, with specific clinical instructions as to how and what physical parts of a man's body she had to manipulate. The erotic imperative was treated as an element quite apart from any emotional or devotional union, so Mangala's directives concerned only the man's pleasure. *His* satisfaction was paramount and Devaki was required to show her gratification, whether felt or not; her art as an actress was therefore indispensable.

~ Won't be difficult to pretend; after all, that's what your abhinaya is no, *acting*? Men are so easily flattered, rājāthi; he'll be a puppet in your hands, you just learn

to pull the right strings, besides pulling other things!
Come come, what's this shyness? You must get used
to bawdy talk. God knows what all he'll say to you.
But I'm telling you, you only have to convince a man
that he is the *best* in some way or another: "Oh you
are so handsome, I'm so lucky to have you …". And
you must moan and cry out as if in ecstasy, "Oh, you
take me to such peaks of pleasure …".
Be inventive, think of things like that to say to him.
Ayyō, so what if you think the opposite, you must
learn to hide your true feelings, I'll tell you this a
hundred times so that you don't forget.

Love for the man she had to pleasure was singularly absent from the induction. If at all any mention was made of emotion, it was that it should *not* intrude into such transactions, was best kept out of it, to enable her to give of her best and make the man feel he was a god. But where *God* was concerned, love was all, *essential*. She was told to serve Him with ardent devotion, bhakti, with all of her being.

There was also practical advice on safety, what herbal pessaries would prevent contraception, how to douche herself after sex to avoid infection and what curative native remedies could help, if she was unfortunate enough to be infected.

Mangala talked to Devaki about her profession, drawing on examples from Indian mythology of semi-divine apsaras: Menaka, Rambha, Urvashi, and

Thilothamma were perfect embodiments of unsurpassed beauty and feminine charms. Besides their sexual expertise, their music and dance entertained divinities and their guests in the court of Lord Indra. This led to the system of guest prostitution, with well-accomplished maidens presented in token of a king's friendship. Trusted ones also acted as spies or messengers. They were also offered as ransom, and often taken as captive slaves by conquerors. Mangala emphasised that devadasis were expected to emulate the comprehensive proficiency of apsaras.

The little devadasi community in backwater Tamil Nadu could not have known that they shared a lot with similar far-flung cultures down the ages, though not necessarily with religious ties: a Japanese oiran, precursor of the geisha, was educated in a range of skills, including the traditional arts of tea ceremony, ikebana and calligraphy. She played instruments and sang; being well-read, she could write poetry and converse with wit and elegance.

Greek hetairai were courtesans, though some also had religious functions. They were renowned for their achievements in dance and music, as well as for their physical and intellectual talents. They were the only women who actively took part in symposia, freely expressing their opinions, much as such participation by 'vésyas', another category of courtesan, was accepted in sabhās. The other similarity was that both groups of women had access to and control over money.

Cortigiana onesta, Venetian courtesans in the sixteenth century were feted and lauded by the city, though their favours were bestowed only on the rich and powerful few. And today's escort services provide the same kind of highly presentable women (or men) capable of being intellectually stimulating, besides being sexually desirable.

###

Kumara visited the Priest quite often and urged Devaki to accompany him, "to fill the gaps in your education that our parents have left". Kumara found the Priest's combination of wide-ranging spiritual knowledge and worldly cynicism fascinating. There was an unspoken kinship between them, that recognition of one aberrant of another. Kumara always had many questions or doubts, which the Priest would answer, sometimes tolerantly, sometimes provocatively. He liked Kumara's lively mind and was entertained by his quick wit that was often equal to parrying his ripostes. Devaki was less enthusiastic about visiting him. Having heard of his reputation, she was wary of him.

- Oo-oh yes, he's a rascal alright. Amma has warned me not to leave you alone with him. Appa is shocked that he's not a "god-fearing man", not bothered about dharma-karma. He compares him to the saintly head priest in Thanjavur, who imparted so much knowledge and guidance to both Amma and Appa. They say he had pads on his ankles as thick as knobs of ginger!

The calloused wads on outer ankle bones indicate how long someone has prayed and meditated sitting in padmasana; similar to the piety bumps on the foreheads of devout Muslims.

- Amma likes to give the impression that she knows all about sex, takes it all in her stride, but do you know, Guruggal told me – with great glee of course – that she didn't know what I am, and that Appa knew more than she did!! Can you believe it, Amma having to be educated by Appa in sexual matters! Oh, I forgot that you're just as ignorant!
- Did Guruggal and Amma …?
- You mean did they have sex? Oh, please ask her; I've always wanted to know! Guruggal is too canny to respond to my hints. They probably did have sex; he's such a randy goat. That's why he had to leave the previous temple.

Oh learning, it is a wonderful thing, but even that couldn't save him! Our Priest prescribed and correctly performed appropriate pujas, recited slokas beautifully, and threw chapter and verse at slack-jawed worshippers. This was a Brahmin who intoned with calm assurance, imbuing his chanting with understanding and appreciation, unlike so many of today's purohits who reel off prayers with such speed, blowing them heavenwards by ripping the aksharas from the mantra, like a hurricane tearing the day's washing off the line.

His erudition was the envy of his peers: this raunchy

profligate could stop any other priest's argument with a laddu – traditional sweetmeat of triumph – of a quotation. If he sensed his superior knowledge was giving them indigestion, he retreated to being as phlegmatic as the rest.

- But his enormous sexual appetite threatened his position. He couldn't leave the local girls alone and his followers gradually stayed away, reducing the temple's income. It must also have been the jealousy of the other priests, that he dared do whatever he wanted to, so openly. I suppose he got tired of all the carping, the hostility. So he decided to move on, and came here. No one to oppose him as he's our only priest. But he finds no mental stimulation here, and though there is still the other kind, looks like he no longer needs *that*. He's now so peppered with pox, and I think he takes opium, so very little matters to him anymore.

###

Devaki shyly raised the topic when she got an opportunity.

- Amma, did you and Guruggal ...?
- Has he been trying to bed you? You be careful; you are not to give in to him, the rascal! Pah, it was different in my case, I had no choice. Fortunately, he soon lost his ruchi for sex: not the stomach ruchi, but in an even more vital organ!
- Was he any different from ... ?

- Well, my patron was more serious, had no time once the sex was over. Ye-es, actually my time with Guruggal was interesting, before he reached this terrible stage. Arrogance, typical arrogance. I suppose he didn't protect himself. He thought he could even stave off the pox with his superior learning! Huh, what use is knowledge if it doesn't make you wise in such basic things that even a fool knows?!

  Of course, I stopped with him as soon as I saw the signs, and that gave me a good excuse to end it. I would have lost my job if I caught the pox, and the temple a source of its income.

  I think he's incapable of anything now, even leaves the village girls alone. Very fortunate for you!
- But what was he like before he became like this? You have to tell me, Amma, if I'm to know all about pleasing men: how and why they are different from each other.
- The strange thing is that Guruggal was the most memorable of my lovers because he could *talk* about such interesting things, he knows so much. Quoted poetry, though the rogue would try and pass off a lot as his own compositions! I was so flattered when he said he'd written a poem for me: "Your breasts are like two kings my dear, Each fighting for the other's sphere".

  I remember that because it's so short. But then your father told me it's a poem by ... some famous poet ... was it Thiruvalluvar? ... I've forgotten ... yes,

Guruggal was that kind of scoundrel, stealing someone else's words.

- *Appa* recognised the poem? I always thought Appa was ignorant of such matters and therefore a bit jealous of Guruggal because of his learning – but if you were also sleeping with him ...
- Nonsense, Appa knew I would go to other men. He just doesn't like Guruggal because he sets a bad example as a Brahmin. He can't help but admire his learning, but feels all that's wasted because of his attitude and behaviour. Appa would love to be learned and has made an effort, though it is not part of his caste. His father learned a lot from his temple priest and passed it on. And also, as you know, the priest of our Thanjavur temple was a wonderfully learned and pious Brahmin, who is Appa's ideal.

The Priest had also found his encounters with Mangala interesting. Not only because she was the only one different from the unwashed illiterate village wenches, but because he found her challenging. She was not cowed by him, was capable of repartee, and used an entertaining turn of speech to mask her ignorance. He could see where Kumara got his characteristics and spirit from. He respected her mind, though that was an uncommon thing in a man of his time.

Their meetings were, therefore, mutually satisfying, not necessarily sexually for Mangala, for whom bedding a man was not something she evaluated on a pleasure scale. No, it was because she had never encountered his like before: vast spiritual knowledge and diverse secular experience that oozed out in worldly-wise ennui. There was something so provocatively entertaining in that unconventional combination. The priest in her old temple was certainly more learned, but he was conservatively predictable and had never expressed such views, or in such a manner.

But while encounters with this Priest were significant, they were also disturbing in some way, leaving Mangala discontented and restless. He, on the other hand, did find the sexual experience stimulating. He also felt a unique lassitude after Mangala drained him. That might have caused a lesser man to feel at a disadvantage, to see himself diminished, weaker than her, as if he were succumbing to the female principle man so dreads. But the Priest would soon resume full control, assert his male superiority and his position*, under which she had to submit.

It might have been some consolation to Mangala to know that women have probably always felt the unnamed depredation she felt. Even if women over the ages were not able to articulate it, the spume of man's lust has never been able to satisfy woman's deep groundswell of desire; the dragging seethe of his thundering brief wave of passion, its ebb leaving her plundered, love's shore eroded. Bereft, that is the universal desolation a woman feels in a sexual relationship in which she feels used, whether whore or wife.

Except in this modern world, when a woman can

choose, use and lose the man, even scornfully paying him for his services. But is that old score thereby settled: do the scales really tip in her favour, or is she left with the same corrosive undertow, a deficit in the measure of love?

###

Lakshmi's torment of Devaki didn't continue for much longer. Kumara was right; Mangala had amassed enough dowry to secure a groom for Lakshmi. She was engaged to Kartikeyan from Chidambaram, son of a 'péria-mélakāran', major musical troupe, definitely a step-up from her father, who was only 'chinna-mélakāran', minor league. Lakshmi boasted that the family belonged to a really important temple, not like *this* insignificant one, suffocated by dry boredom, like its scrub and rock. She looked forward to be going to a big city, where there would be so much to do and see. Though she secretly wondered how much of the city she would be able to enjoy, as her betrothed lived on his land some way out of the city, for he had reverted to his community's original 'vellalar' occupation of agriculture. Some sons of 'mélakāran' turned to other occupations if they felt themselves unsuited to music.

Lakshmi finally had her moment of glory with a suitably lavish wedding. As he once did with Lakshmi, Kumara had now to persuade Devaki to help in preparations and participate wholeheartedly in the celebrations. As the bride's brother, he had an important role to play, welcoming the groom's party, seeing them comfortably settled and properly fed. After the wedding, he would accompany Lakshmi to her new home and was looking forward to visiting that renowned city.

Kumara decided he would spare the half-starved pony the burden of the groom's weight; instead, Kumara persuaded him to walk the short distance to the temple, where the bride and her family waited. The groom's bulk made for more than customary slow progress – oh, Kumara was going to regale the family later, with his observations about him!

A traditional band led the procession. Village or barber's bands were only for secular celebrations. They were called "German bands" if their western instruments were mainly metal. Ensembles of blaring brass, drums and large cymbals, sometimes woodwind as well, were capable of robust renditions of any tune they heard. They could play by ear anything to suit the occasion, from a celebratory "For he's a Jolly Good Fellow", to a Scottish reel for a joyous function, to the "Funeral March" on the way to the cemetery. Even today these bands exist, leading the bridegroom's procession to the wedding venue, "Come September" being a staple.

###

After a tearful farewell to Lakshmi, Mangala could devote all her attention to Devaki. She sighed over the fact that Devaki's proficiency had reached a plateau. No,

Devaki was not going to get any better as a dancer, but her unusual beauty would serve well. The puja to consecrate her anklet bells was held to mark the conclusion of her dance training. Mangala missed Lakshmi when decorating the house and seeing to all the preparations, though of course Kumara was, as ever, an eager helper.

The nattuvanār conducted a navagraha puja to sanctify the performing space. Devaki's new dance costume and ankle bells were added to the auspicious platter which was taken around for all the invited elders and aficionados to touch in blessing. Mangala placed the ankle bells in front of the family deity and Devaki touched the feet of the guru who tied the bells to her feet. He was presented with his fee and honoured with presents. As a sign of her competence, she was allowed, for the first time, to dance with ankle bells, to full musical accompaniment.

Five days later, an 'acchu', silver impress, branded her thigh with Shiva's trident, setting the seal on her as the temple devadasi. Mangala would apply herbal packs to the burned area till it healed.

###

The 'sadanku' marked a devadasi's onset of puberty, confirmed her status as an accomplished dancer and full-fledged temple employee, and was a symbolic marriage of the pubescent Devaki to the temple's deity. After Lakshmi's extravagant wedding, funds were scarce for the ceremony. Nattuvanār had to be rewarded for imparting his valued knowledge, and the Priest also named a price for giving the girl the honour of serving the Lord.

To ensure ritual purity of the auspicious occasion, Devaki fasted, and the house was rendered pollution-free for days. Kumara had put his best aesthetic considerations into decorating the wedding platform. It was framed by banana stems wound with strings of flowers. Further swags of flowers adorned the ceremonial canopy. Brass and silver items shone with the application of ash, tamarind, coir husk and elbow grease. Neem leaves overflowed from the mouth of the round water pot signifying fertility. Platters of fruits and coconuts with other puja necessities were ranged around the mané, flanked by two oil lamps and kōlams bordered all these auspicious items.

The band of musicians processed to the temple with menopausal women taking presents to the 'utsava murthi', the idol bridegroom, and a gold-edged 'véshti' for the priest. They returned with the mangalsutra and a new sari and blouse for the bride. Puja items and the 'kattari' (the deity's emblem or substitute was a sword wound with flowers, its tip covered with a lime), were placed in the sacramentally cleansed room.

After the auspicious cleansing of a ritual bath, Devaki changed into her new clothes, then faced more ceremonies. She sat fully clothed while older women poured water over her through a sieve, signifying the benediction of rain. Turmeric was smeared over her face and vibhuthi on her forehead. She stood on the platform, facing north, the 'kattari' held in her right hand while her wedding was performed, identical to a traditional non-Brahmin one. After the ārathi, the golden mangalsutra was tied around her neck and she was smeared with sandalwood paste, to mark her marital status.

In the meantime, nattuvanār sanctified the dance platform for her debut, 'aranga', a raised platform or stage which she ascends. The guests – among them the wealthy and connoisseurs – would judge both teacher and taught. Her talent and proficiency were a reflection of the guru's skill in imparting that knowledge to her. This first step in the traditional mārgam, the path that reflects the stages of the dancer's consciousness, also officially qualified her to dance in the temple, though her repertoire was still limited, without much abhinaya.

In the evening, in a new sari draped over her dance pyjama, she was taken to the temple for her first duties. The Priest tied the red cloth, symbol of her position, around her head and gave her prasadam. She performed a special arathi before her performance. While guests feasted on special food, she was allowed only milk and fruit. After the kumbha-deepam, a devadasi's special duty, she received gifts and blessings, and the musicians escorted her back to the house, a new bride who had to enter the nuptial bed that night to "consummate her marriage" with the decorated sword.

Though Devaki felt faint with the fasting, heat and emotion, she had to endure more rituals which were replicas of regular weddings. 'Nalanku', suggestive songs that urged sexual coupling, and 'lāli', lullabies, were sung. Shanti-homa was said in front of the nuptial bed, where she lay next to the 'kattari' and "gave of her embryo" to it, the symbolic intercourse replacing a regular bride's "deflowering". She would then be soulmate of god, wedded to his mental image rather than any material substitute.

The next morning, Mangala and the other women took the kattari-bridegroom back to the temple in a procession after which the community celebrated the unison of heaven and earth, from which the life cycle of rain, fertility and abundance would follow. After a ritual bath Devaki was allowed to break her fast. Kumara had ordered her favourite dish, idlis, to fortify her, as there was more ritual and dancing, after which she would have a respite of a few days. Fortunately for her, this temple wasn't wealthy enough to support the twelve-day festivities that normally followed the wedding, in which the bride had to dress as a different goddess each day, with more music and dance and clamour.

###

The 'prayojanam' marked the actual sexual consummation with a patron, 'puravalar'. The ceremony was widely advertised in the hope of attracting prospective patrons, whose offers would be vetted. The richest usually won, for he had to bear the ceremony's costs and the privilege of maintaining the devadasi thereafter. This sexual arrangement was justified because of the devadasi's divine status that was a means for the secular lover to be united with god. It was her "dedicated" status that crucially made her a symbol of social prestige. After all, merely sexual pleasures could be bought from any "kept woman".

> [Promila: I find it particularly repellent that baby girls were sold or "given" to become sex slaves. Let's face it, that's what devadasis were.
> Fiona: Yes, yet another example of Hindu sophistry that also justifies erotic sculpture, the Kamasutra etc etc. in the same way: "sex is one means of union of individual soul with the divine".
> Bhaumi: But Promila, sacred prostitution existed in other societies as well, from the Near East all the way across to Meso and South America. The Greek sacrament of the 'hieros gamos' was witnessed and blessed by the Gods, as it was regarded as a reunion of the souls of the two lovers becoming the Original Unity.
> Promila: Bottom line, baby girls being sold or given to become devadasis is violation of human rights. It's child abuse!
> Akhil: But using children for personal gain has always taken many forms: slavery, sold during famine or in times of financial desperation ....
> Rishab: ... and continues even now to sex traffickers.

Promila: So all that is justified?
Advik: No, of course not, but I guess when so little premium is put on all life, humans are seen as just another material possession, to use and dispense with, by whoever owns them or has power over them.]

###

Usually the mother and grandmother chose the patron and came to a satisfactory and lucrative arrangement with him. After a month, the girl could decide for herself if she wanted to continue in the relationship, or end it after a stipulated time: another example of the comparative freedom a devadasi had over her life. If the man abandoned her, there was not only the financial safety net of the community, her profession also allowed her to seek another patron. A month didn't seem long enough for Devaki to decide who her patron would be and for how long, though she knew Mangala would steer her in the most expedient direction.

She dreaded the next step: her union with the god over, it now had to be consummated with a mortal lover. Kumara teased her about her new status:

- Your bells are not only tell-tales when you make dance mistakes. They will give you away when Amma ties them on at afternoon rest-time, to make sure you don't go out. She's warned me, "No more loafing with her. Her status has changed." It's going to be so boring for me, not even Lakshmi here to limp around with me.

- Boring for *you* Annan, what about *me*, lying down in a dark room!? Why, can't you sit with me and play 5-stones or some other game?
- *Games?!* You'll have other kinds of games with your patron, darling, wait and see! That is, when you aren't dancing.

###

Kumara was right. Devaki hated the extended hours of practice. Her guru was oblivious of time so that classes went on for hours, till she begged for a break. He now concentrated on the next stages of the mārgam, the evolution of a dancer's consciousness to elevate her to her true goal of divine representative. He aspired to train both ear and heart to exercise and cultivate her imagination and piety.

He had no fixed syllabus or teaching methodology, so relied on improvisation. His cultural matrix and racial memory made him intuitive in teaching. He taught students as much by what he said as by what he did not say. This frustrated Devaki when she could not decipher what her guru left unsaid.

The nattuvanār's position waned somewhat, though it was not obliterated as sharply as the devadasi's. He found himself in demand as a teacher, though in the modern arena he lacked the social savvy and PR skills to chase fame and lobby for patronage or sponsorship. Once his secular pupils mastered what he imparted, he often lost his exclusive control over such personal heritage, his role being taken over by a younger generation of dancers who were not part of his tradition.

In the heyday of his profession, the nattuvanār's life and art were Siamese twins, giving him advantages over modern dance gurus, who have to prove that they are worthy of their fees. Parents often pressurise them to arrange an early (premature) debut, seeking success for their children in a competitive world. Some modern gurus have a production belt of students, cloned with an unvaried syllabus, so that creativity in laya, which requires unhurried reflection, is impossible.

The traditional nattuvanār had no such compulsions. Since he did not perform on stage, he could focus all his energies on the student. There was no competitiveness, or the fear of the student overtaking the master. His success depended upon hers. His livelihood secure and without the burden of rivalry, he had the leisure to innovate and give individual attention to each pupil. Nothing was copied or cloned, as is the norm today. Variations were usually inspired by the framework of a dancer's nature, personality and technical abilities, and some of the best compositions often sprung up thus spontaneously. As she matured in her art, self-criticism and creativity were fostered in a dedicated dancer, exciting her imagination.

The nattuvanār transformed the splendour of temple visuals of legends and myths into emotionally imbued bhava, modes of expression, not the dry narratives we see today. So keen on innovation are some modern choreographer-dancers that they dig up obscure poems and devotional songs to create new dances. Their nritta passages appear as if mathematically calculated and, as if their stamina needed to be proved, are distended rather than extended. Devaki's guru was neither interested in such shows of endurance, nor was Devaki equal to them. He felt she was more capable of communicating repose, 'laya', therefore concentrated on the visual patterns to bring it out, interspersed with only brief bursts of 'tirmanams', energetic steps.

'Laya' relied heavily on abhinaya and the nattuvanār imparted all instruction while seated, using only his face and hands to convey the expression or emotion desired. Here Mangala was of great help as it was easier for a woman to demonstrate the essentially feminine experiences of abhinaya. Elaborating with metaphor and idiom, they emphasised how important it was to create the illusion of the sculptured goddess coming alive to dance to the music. Explications of the cultural background of a varnam or padam also gave Mangala excuses to give Devaki desperately desired breaks.

- As you are teaching Devaki that varnam, don't you think it would help if we tell her about what we were discussing the other day, about the different aspects of Krishna? Rājāthi, come sit here. In this piece you are the nayaki waiting for her lover, so express her longing, sadness like this ....

- Yes Mangala, but it is never *only* about that kind of love. Devaki, you also have to bring out the larger meaning, that the jivatma is longing for union with the paramatma.
- But the lyrics are short, so sentiments have to be conveyed quickly ....
- As long as there are no more strenuous adavus. My feet are really hurting.
- Don't be silly Devaki, nritta has to accompany 'sollu kattu'. Aciriyar will keep them simple and short.

###

Not that her other professional requirements were any easier. She had regularly to dance in the temple and master those pujas required of her. A temple encapsulates time and space, its deity housed in the garbha griha, sacred womb sheltered from all the elements. From this still centre, rituals performed by intermediaries – priests and devadasis – draw out the correct vibrations to preserve world order. Only precision in their performance resulted in the required balance and stability, benefits they then bestowed on lay worshippers. Devaki had to control her nervousness at such onerous responsibility, being careful not to falter.

Some relief from physical exertion came when studying Telegu and Kannada in addition to mandatory Tamil, to elaborate the context of the songs to which she danced. Listening to the mythical stories and legends that were woven into padams or varnams was also welcome diversion from laborious training.

8

~ Yén-gō, I'm a little nervous now that Devaki is having her 'prayojanam' today. Of course, I've instructed her in how her consummation with an actual partner will be ....

~ Then why worry, Mangala? She has to carry out her duties, you've trained her all these years ....

~ Yes, as long as she obeys me in all that I've told her to do. She's shy in some ways, but is so impulsive, without thinking of the consequences.

~ She's still really a child ....

~ This defiant streak in her, she must get it from her mother. Pah, that Kamala was a rebel, always wanted her own way. That poor Velu hadn't a clue.

~ Don't let Devaki hear a word about "her parents". You

are an 'ōtaivai', such a blabbermouth, you'd better watch it.

Devaki's first assignment with her 'puravalar' was followed by identical ones at regular intervals. On their afternoon explorations, the children had sometimes raided the wealthy landowner's fruit trees and speculated about the riches of the grand house they could see but never dared approach, despite Devaki's curiosity and Kumara's daring. Mangala had told them about similar houses she had visited in her heyday, when she had to dance for them. Most of them followed a traditional pattern.

The main rooms of the house opened onto a large courtyard exposed to the sky, surrounded by a pillared corridor, to shelter the rooms from sun and rain. Women set grains, chillies and papads to dry in the courtyard, or sat around cleaning rice and dhal, providing them opportunities for quarreling or bitching, chat or banter. Outside the kitchen, a partially covered area housed a block of granite with a round depression for pounding grain into flour, stones for grinding masala, and the quern. When the stones were worn too smooth, the 'vaddera' or stonecutter, was called in to chip the surfaces to roughen them again.

The living room was the largest and gave way to the front door in its south wall, opening onto a porch with stone slabs for seats, where the visitor who could not be admitted into the house could meet the owner. The men of the house could also sit there of an evening, watching the street activity. Indoors, mats were unfurled when people wanted to sit down, that also served as beds in poorer households. Pictures and idols in the puja room were garlanded and smeared with sandalwood paste, kumkum and turmeric, and the scent of exhausted agarbathi clung to the walls.

There was a "visitor's room", elaborately furnished with western furniture, chairs and sofas protected with antimacassars (given the Indian's proclivity for hair oil, such precaution was not amiss), fancy tables protected with doilies (testament to the crochet, embroidery and other handiwork of the women of the household), and display cabinets showing off bric-a-brac; all western of course – porcelain figurines, crystal bowls, silver knick-knacks – as collecting Indian artefacts and antiques was not yet in fashion. Those who wished further to assert their more "westernized liberal" leanings, even had paintings or marble statues of naked women. This room was kept shuttered and closed, used only to receive important dignitaries or foreign guests.

###

Devaki delighted in alankāra, adornment and ornamentation, of both the deity and herself. Though she sometimes protested:

- Amma, why must I wear all this jewellery and 'pattu-vastram', these heavy gold brocade saris when 'puravalar' comes? Look at these stone goddesses around us, they wear hardly any clothes!

- Āhahā, what, like them you also want to go around with transparent clothes to show your breasts and that flimsy cloth around your waist? Actually, it always makes me laugh: those figures are often seen without clothes but never without jewellery!
- Lucky them: in this heat, it must be so comfortable to wear so little!
- We devadasis have a secret: the more you cover yourself up, the more the man exercises his imagination. It's erotic for him to fantasise about what's under all this, what all he'll have to take off before he gets to his destination!
- Pōngō Amma, always talking about such things ....
- Then what? Speak about crops and taxes to a woman of pleasure, or what?

Mangala's "secret" accorded with Abbe Dubois' perceptive observation of devadasis: "They are particularly careful not to expose any part of the body. Experience has no doubt taught them that for a woman to display her charms damps sensual ardour, instead of exciting it, and that the imagination is more easily captivated than the eye", which makes me wonder what that man of God saw in his mind's eye!

###

The patron's regular visits made him no more tolerable to Devaki, and she still chafed* in her distasteful role.

- What's the matter, Devaki? You are so restless and it isn't even your "outside time" yet.
- I was made to do things I don't like.
- 'Puruvalar' has paid for you and you will have to do whatever pleases him, whatever he wants of you sexually. It is your duty.
- Oh, and I thought my *duty* was to *God*!
- What rubbish, Devaki. As if I haven't told you the patron owns you. You just have to bear it.

[Sagarika: The poor girl must have turned schizophrenic, having to fulfill these irreconcilable functions with equal sincerity!
Advik: That's Hindusim for you: under the guise of reconciling dualities to enable you to reach the Ultimate Reality, it has all these contradictions conveniently explained away by sophistry.
Promila: Why should a devadasi sleep with a mortal, making her – who is so "auspicious, sacred, the best offering to god" blah blah blah – nothing more than a prostitute?
Fiona: And how come sex with an ordinary man – whose only qualification is that he can pay enough for her – doesn't pollute her for her primary temple duties?
Promila: And I want to know why they needed to sleep with men at all?

SD: In the past, rajas supported temples completely. Without concerning herself about a livelihood, the devadasi could devote her time, energy and attention to the rigorous physical discipline and study demanded to fulfil her original role. But as that patronage diminished, the temple alone couldn't provide her sufficient financial sustenance. She was forced to take patrons. In one sense, you could see the upside of her position: she was free of the control that husbands exert over their wives, and she wasn't confined to a home life, with all its distractions of domesticity.]

- Amma, pah, sometimes he's drunk and stinks ....
- *Never* show revulsion, displeasure, pain or boredom. I've told you, suppress all feelings. And doesn't your main duty already give you all the pleasure and satisfaction you need? You are a dancer to our God first, apart from your other duties to Him.

  But in a way, the two masters, God and man, are not a conundrum. Look at the way our dance blends sensuality and divinity. Go and talk to Guruggal; he'll tell you how our Puranas are full of stories about how lusty our gods were.

  Our erotic form of dance is meant not only to titillate men; our gods also enjoy being aroused by them. We've told you, you dance for God, to keep auspiciousness in the temple, so your dance must be perfect to have the desired effect.

Master your precious art while you still can.

I know now, with my little knowledge of the shastras – and vaster one of men – what I have been trying to express for years through my dance. How ironic; now my body lets me down and can no longer convey what is in my heart, and what my mind knows! That is the only shackle a dancer suffers: when her ageing body refuses to take flight with her heart-mind.

By the way, Guruggal wants to see you. He's not satisfied with your dancing. Frankly, I'm surprised he even notices such things. He seems to be in another world, though that is not necessarily the one above!

Devaki was surprised when her father detained her after Mangala left. He seldom spoke to her, though she sensed his affection. As Kumara said, he was an undemonstrative man; but he was loved by the children, and respected by all – after all, he could keep the spirited Mangala in check! One sensed his quiet reserves of integrity and strength.

~ Amma has given you a lot of advice but I would also like to speak my mind. Your dance. I feel your heart isn't in it. To be the best, you really have to *love* what you do.

~ What I *have* to do, Appa.

~ Don't we all, *have* to do? The males in our community, what choice do we have? We are second class citizens with women having the upper hand. We *have* to become musicians or dance teachers. I sometimes dream of a small plot of land by the river, in a house where I can hear the sound of the water. Grow enough rice to feed ourselves, a cow in the backyard … Instead, I am a tenant in Mangala's house. So, it is my fate to live off women.

I know you don't get much from your 'puravalar', he pays the temple directly. So how can I ask for a portion of the sari he gives you for Pongal or the bangles he slides on your arm?

- Oh Appa, as if my yearning is just for jewellery and clothes! No! Why do I feel that somewhere between the shastras and the beautiful poems and the heroic tales, there is something *missing* in my dance, in my *life*?
- Much of what you say is true. Your Amma also felt that way many times, but she turned her mind and heart away, turned them to God in fact, when she had to do what she felt was unpalatable. That is the only way.
- I see the smile on the faces of these disporting divinities on these walls and feel that *they* know what is missing, the secret is frozen on their lips, in their tantalizing smiles. What is it?
- It is pity for us mortals, wanting so much, always reaching out for something else …. They smile because they are beyond desire, results, dualities ... all the things Krishna teaches us in the Gita. All that is beyond this worldly frippery.

And it is a great pity that a devadasi has also become just one more plaything. In times past, your role had so much meaning! Now the devadasi has strayed far from that pure service, forever desecrating her role divine, sabotaging that heaven.

Lust and greed have replaced faith and piety, while we worship a new material god in carnal festivities, instead of sacred celebrations.

Amma said the Priest wants to see you? I think he wants to give you some background about your role. I just hope he will also give you an idea of its *seriousness,* in addition to the salacious details I'm sure he won't omit.

###

Shankara was right. The Priest's conversation with Devaki was spiced with enlightening – but not necessarily edifyingly *vital* – information. Kumara was sent along as spy and censor, though he was too distracted by the Priest's revelations to fulfil either role.

~ Devaki, I'm sure your Amma has instructed you in your physical role with your 'puravalar'. Well, who better to give you such advice. And your Appa? Hmm, I suppose he went on about your godly duty, dharma, morality, all those *good* things ... so, let me tell you other stories about our gods, devatas, rishis – all our *good* men, mind you! You must have already heard about those glorious apsaras ....

~ Oh yes, I've heard about Menaka, Urvashi ....

~ Yes, yes, you are part of their tradition, so you know

all about being good at dancing, singing, reciting poetry, sex … but *their* original roles involved much more: be thankful that you don't have to go on some of their missions!

When our jealous gods saw that rishis were doing severe penance and acquiring supernatural faculties, to safeguard their monopoly on such powers, women were used to unleash the gods' two favourite weapons: kama-krōdha, desire and ire.

Oh yes, our gods knew all about passion and wrath because they were often prey to them! And imagine how incensed sages became when, after undergoing years of severe penance to control the senses, they found they were aroused, that they hadn't conquered their lasciviousness! Ha ha ha! So easily undone by itch and fury. Poooof, gone years of tapas; whoosh, gone accrued tejas. Oh, I do love stories of those irate worthies spewing curses when their accumulated powers, the result of decades of devoted deprivation and sacrifice were blown away by the mere waft of a damsel's diaphanous garment!

Or worse than cursing, when those good men – gods and sages – displayed unbecoming incontinence by "aimlessly spilling their seed". No, Hindu narrative certainly didn't hold back!* According to one version of Agasthya's birth, Mitra and Varuna were both rejected when competing for Urvashi's favours. Since their arousal was thwarted from its appropriate expression, they discharged it into a clay pot (thereby giving a whole new meaning to the term tosspots*). The boy born from the pitcher found floating in the Ganga was named Kumbha-sambhava, pot-born.

God Kumar's birth gives rise to two of his other names. Skanda perhaps derives from 'skandr', ooze or leap: Shiva spilt his seed in premature ejaculation when his love-making with Parvathi was interrupted. His semen was carried by the river Ganga to a pond, resulting in Saravana, "born amongst the reeds", another name for Karthikeya. Though another version replaces semen with fire from Shiva's third eye: Choose your preferred anatomical* interpretation!

- But Guruggal, if women are so wicked, why do we worship goddesses?
- Āhahā, Kumara, so you would like to do away with women altogether? Women to be worshipped or reviled? That is the problem with our stories, so many inconsistencies and contradictions. Some claim that woman is evil, created only to corrupt man. While another story has it that man was lonely. 'Path' means "lord" but also means "to fall away". So, from a part of man, god created a wife: 'pâth-ni'. Rather like the Christian story of Adam and Eve.

Interesting these parallels, not only that God created woman since man was lonely, but that man had first to lose a part of himself, so that he could take unto himself a partner (even the English word contains *part*). For if one is already whole, how can one take on another part?

Most Hindu schools of thought believe that the Original Egg split into purusha and prakriti, the dormant male and the active female. How very apt: the male's member can function and discharge* its duty only if the female stimulates it. So goddesses – Shakti, active power – are the necessary halves of gods. But Shakti can be benevolent or malignant. The goddess' smile can also conceal a Kali thirsty for blood; blood that is needed for fertility and regeneration. In many ancient societies blood-letting and copulation were believed to bring rain and fertility.

[Advik: There seem to be such contradictory views about blood. It was considered auspicious in sacrifice, a sign of fertility. But blood was also considered polluting?
Promila: Maybe it was only menstrual blood that was polluting?
Fiona: Could it be because menses is the womb's disappointed discard, the very opposite of fertility?
Bhaumi: Yes, therefore inauspicious!
Advik: Surely primitive man didn't shy away from blood? After all, it was very much part of his hunting life, and also in ritual sacrifice.
Promila: So at what point in "civilization" did man seclude woman during menses, claiming her blood was unclean? Or was menses seen as something erotic and therefore the reason for her seclusion?

Fiona: I think it was a combination of seeing blood as unclean and seeing it as the power of fertility and fecundity.

Akhil: The same concept of pollution exists in most religions. Till recently even Christians didn't want women priests. Catholics still don't ordain them. Is a woman's body too unclean to be at the altar, serving god directly?]

'Purusha-medha' – if indeed human sacrifice was actual and not purely symbolic – was gradually replaced with animal offerings.

- Temples like ours no longer practice blood sacrifices but there are many 'idangai', left-handed, temples that do, usually offering buffaloes or goats; the poorer ones sacrifice chickens. When Brahmins became 'saivam', gave up killing animals and eating meat, they modified those old customs, so that kumkum is used instead of blood.
- You mean I would have had *blood* smeared on my forehead? Chee!
- Yes Devaki, particularly for women, blood signified fertility.

Over time, other less gory replacements were made. A coconut, its "eyes" emphasising its anthropomorphic substitution, is now broken instead of someone's skull. Or a white pumpkin is smashed and then smeared with vermilion, so that it really does look like someone's head cracked open, full of blood.

[Bhaumi: Oh, maybe that is why in Bengal, where I come from, women are not supposed to cut open pumpkins!]

- Why would we want to be reminded of such a brutal past, Guruggal?
- You think it's all the past Kumara? No, it continues even now.

[SD: And even now, I believe some Tantrics and other Bhairavamurthy cults still practise human sacrifice. Don't look so shocked, my dear young listeners, but yes, it is said to happen even today. In the Ammanathan temple near Tiruneveli, its fearsome deity, Sudalai Madan, was banished to earth for his preference for eating human flesh over amrith. To divert the deity's wrath from their community, Kaniyans perform human sacrifice, dancing in graveyards, looking for corpses and even gnawing bones! Though they claim they no longer practise human sacrifice, witnesses have reported otherwise.]

- Guruggal, no wonder they say Kaliyuga is upon us!
- All the smoke from ritual fires and our sacred chants, they are trying to stay the ever-advancing, ever-increasing oppressive effects of Kaliyuga.

- But Guruggal, aren't we supposed to be saved by Kalki, the last avatar?
- Hmm, so Kumara, who do you think this Kalki is? Saviour from destruction, or its harbinger? Is he the Titan shouldering heaven's wrath, to prevent it from crashing down on wicked earth? The prayers we poor mortals send heavenwards help him bear his load. But hairline cracks have appeared in the Titan's vertebrae, his joints crepitate, ankylosed with the weight of Kaliyuga's evil, so that it is only a matter of time before he collapses under god's outrage, no longer able to avert earth's obliteration.

  Is Kalki the avatar to bear us beyond the end of this evil yuga's destruction; he who rides in on a white horse, holding back pralaya, dissolution, till the chosen moment? Or is Kalki the eschaton mare itself, fire at the bottom of the ocean that will one day leap forth to destroy the world?

Hindu legend believes that the oceans cover the earth's fiery core, keeping its energy and heat at bay; a fire-mare that is restricted by its promise to Saraswathi to drink the oceans' waters through a mouth no larger than a needle head. Doomsday could well be a fiery eruption, the earth's boiling core in the ocean that finally consumes the earth, ending Kaliyug. Beware the tsunami, beware the Year of the Fire Horse!

- But Gurggal, you told me that Vishnu avatars came on earth both to destroy it *and* save it; that only with pralaya could the next yuga be created, no?

~ Oh, well done Kumara, you paid attention to my stories! That is true, though it is uncertain if there will be another yuga, another throw of the dice, for Kalki is, after all, the last avatar. Maybe there can be no greater evil than what we are experiencing in this yuga.

Yes children, here's more evidence of Kaliyuga: there's a tribe that sacrifices a boy, whose blood ensures that the turmeric they grow has a rich red colour, highly sought after.

But the victim must always be purchased. And because the villagers have paid a price for him, they feel no sin attaches to *them* for killing him, the sin then being that of the parents for selling him to be sacrificed.

When I was a child I heard the most gruesome story of them all. This tribe buys a human, usually an infant boy, and brings him up. When it is time for him to become a 'merai', the sacrifice, they hobble him by breaking his legs and parade him through the village in an open cart. All the villagers touch the oil on his head and put it on their own foreheads as a blessing. The boy I heard about, at the sacrificial pit, chunks of his back were hacked off – while he was alive – and the villagers ran to their fields to bury the flesh, believing it would enrich their land and guarantee a good harvest. Then they ....

~ Ayyō ayyō, please please Guruggal *stop*, I beg you! Why are you telling us such horrible things? I'm going to be sick ....

- Alright, I'll spare you two young innocents of other such practices.

Such as 'ashva-médha', where the queen had sexual intercourse with the sacrificial horse; whether the animal was alive or dead is another moot point. Over time, such sexual union was probably substituted by a young girl performing symbolic intercourse with the deity.

It was a short step to sacred harlotry: the priest was 'bhūdeva', a godling on earth. Just as he had first claim to anything offered to god, so also could he first partake of the proffered girl. A functionary to the gods, but oh so many human perks* in being a priest! The Brahmin gladly stepped in as the deity's substitute.

Defloration – whether on the symbol of the deity such as the ithyphallic idol or sword, or with the priest – also meant blood from the ruptured hymen; only god or the priest could negate its polluting attributes. Brahmins with agendas no doubt justified many such practices that in time became "established".

After the priest, it was but a short step to the raja – god's secular representative, responsible for his kingdom's stability and prosperity, much as god was for the universe – then claiming his pound of flesh*. Power games led to priests not only appropriating this right but also passing the right on to the officials or other men of power such as rajas, landlords, hence 'droit de seigneur', when the owner had the right to have sex with those who worked for him. So, prerogatives on her body filtered down the pecking* order to rich patrons, whether landowners or merchants, and finally the market place.

From service to God with an honourable art that incidentally also brought her wealth and power, her fall parallels that of the establishment she served. The temple was gradually beset with the shortcomings of all man-made institutions – greed, corruption, ego struggles, power-politics – and the god-business was, and continues to be, exploited accordingly. Religion is no guarantee of moral sanctity or spirituality; in fact, those defining tenets seem to decrease inversely when faith hardens into institutional intolerance.

Though the British denounced the devadasi system as immoral and bawdy, some were not above having nautch as entertaining erotica at their dinner gatherings. That hypocrisy didn't prevent social reform from banning dance from temples. With the loss of her original livelihood, the devadasi's descent into moral squalor was complete.

###

Devaki was negatively spoiled for choice: did she hate her sexual duty more, or her hours of service in the temple, underpinned as that was with hours of dance practice and other lessons?

- Annan, I just can't take it any more. What am I? I'm just a *sex servant* to my patron, that stinky brute, not his wife. And in every way I'm a slave to God, not his wife either. I clean the puja vessels, do ārathi, dance, do whatever I'm told are His wishes, but that doesn't make me His *wife*. What I mean is, I don't do that *important thing* wives do for their husbands, you know ....

- Oh come on Devaki, can't you at least say *sex*, if not the cruder word I use? Yeah, all you got was the 'kattari' on your wedding night! What a con! But at least you got deflowered later by a young, not bad-looking guy. Stinky brute? Come on, even I wouldn't mind a go with him! You're lucky it wasn't the Priest; they usually have first go, being representatives of the deity and all that. Thank god our randy Priest is now too poxed to be able to do anything. I wonder if he used to give Amma a hard time. "*Hard* time", get it?!
- Chee, Annan, stop it. I can't even have a proper discussion with you. I'm serious. Why am I called God's *wife*? Amma is of no help when I want to discuss such things. To nearly all my questions she says, "It's sanctioned, it's your duty." You said she learned so much when she was in Thanjavur, so why can't she give me a proper answer?
- I think Guruggal has put doubts in her mind and she's no longer confident in what she once believed. She greatly admired Guruggal's mind. They used to have long discussions. She probably no longer feels comfortable with those beliefs she once had. She doesn't need you to go digging up her doubts again. Let's go and ask Guruggal. He hides all he knows under all that pretence of being beyond caring about anything.

###

- Remember Guruggal, you once talked to me about marriage? So why is Devaki married to a God with whom the sexual act is not possible? Why not just call her what she actually is, a slave who works for him?
- But that is exactly what she is: *servant* to God, not wife.
- Okay Guruggal, even if a devadasi is a servant who belongs to the deity, to serve him, to do his bidding, why did the notion of sex enter?
- You know we see the world in polarities, evolution/dissolution, eternal/temporal, polluting/auspicious, heating/cooling ... even foods are classified and prescribed according to the seasons. Everything is to be done in the correct way and at the correct time according to our shastras, whether it is what clothes to wear, when the flag is to be hoisted, or which direction you should face to ....
- ... fart?
- I don't think that category is covered, actually Kumara. I was going to say "to do a certain puja". It's our usual fondness for classifications: desire is "heating", dangerous even in gods. Remember Shiva's penance? He had accumulated so much tejas he could burn Kama to ashes with a glance. And if Mariamma gets heated, small pox breaks out, drought, famine .... Permanent celibacy is not a desired condition, with lust and frustration building up, physically, mentally and emotionally.

It is the woman who pours water on man's fire. Heat

has to be balanced out with what is "cooling". In the case of sexual passion of man, that heat has to be drawn off by the woman.

- But doesn't God have his divine wives to cool his fires? And why do I have to do that for a *patron*, when he has his own wife to do it? I don't even mind "drawing it out" for god, but for a man …?
- Oh-ho, "drawing it out"?! Developing Kumara's humour are you, Devaki? Ah, we men have always needed more than one woman. We are but following the example of our gods and heroes … Krishna, Arjuna. As above, so below. God is the divine king, or the king is god on earth, see it how you will. The raja is the divine king's mortal counterpart, his representative on earth. So our kings have God's responsibilities in earthly form. It is also the other way around: God has to be treated like a king. So he is given costly clothes, jewels, chariots in which he can be taken out in procession. But because a devadasi serves God, she also has to serve the king. Then her services gradually got demoted to zamindars, rich landlords, now even merchants and traders ….
- … And don't leave out priests!
- Yes Kumara, quite right. Priests have priority before those others because he is God's servant and as his payment, he takes whatever is offered to his master.
- But men are so possessive about their wives. Men wouldn't share *them* with any other men! Why do gods?

- Because they *have* so many? Must be exhausting for a god, what Guruggal?
- But I'm *married* to *God*! How can God bear to *share* his *wife* with mere mortals, when a mere mortal doesn't do so?
- Doesn't He share you with us in other ways? When you dance for God, don't we enjoy your dance? And prasadam and flowers, after offering them to God, don't we take them? Why? Because they are blessed by Him. In fact, when He shares *you* – His most treasured possession – you are the most auspicious for us, whether in the ārathis you perform, your dance, or your body.

  Everything, everyone, has an allotted function. Just like dance requires tala and raga for each specific occasion. Dance and music are among the temple rituals to entertain and please the deity. Nataraja danced to bring about balance and cosmic order; your dance maintains it. I've told you, it's all about ensuring balance. Women are needed to cool man's passion. Women don't need men to heat them up, they don't need heat even from a God.

[Promila: So that's the excuse men have for promiscuity? They need to have their "heat drawn out"? So why isn't woman allowed to spread her largesse around by sleeping with several men, "drawing out their heat"?

Rishab: But I've heard that there were male

counterparts of devadasis: how does the "temperature equation" apply to sex between two males?

SD: This is another example where things can't be explained wholly satisfactorily, except perhaps that *any* form of male sexual release is a ridding of the undesirable accumulation of "heating" passion, which adversely affects both body and mind.

Bhaumi: But, as usual, that explanation is such a convenient cop-out, dodging the problem. If devadasis were so necessary to maintain cosmic order, did the world start deteriorating only after they were banished from temples?

SD: Well, I guess some would explain that away as the increasing effects of kaliyug. I'm just playing devil's advocate here, okay? When devadasis were allowed to fulfil their proper functions, it was in the early stages of kaliyug, so their role coincided with the comparative goodness that existed. Their loss of status and function now parallels the rapid deterioration wrought by kaliyug; just more evidence of its increasing evil.]

9

Albert Long, ambitious Assistant Magistrate, enjoyed life in Madras so he disliked the touring his post involved. On one such tour of duty, he was deputed to investigate suspiciously large claims of land by the temple to which Devaki was attached. Pleading ill-health, the Priest dodged Albert's summons, so that Albert was obliged to go to the temple to question him and examine his documents. The day was particularly hot, making his ride extremely uncomfortable, and his mood was not improved by the slippery explanations of the canny Priest that led Albert into further by-ways of doubt. Albert couldn't unearth the jobbery he knew lurked somewhere, and rode away with the irritating impression that the Priest was laughing up his sleeve at his official impotence.

Perhaps to avenge himself at being upstaged, Albert casually mentioned to his bearer, John, that he'd glimpsed a girl at the temple. Albert, aware of John's resourcefulness, knew a hint was enough for him. On his part, John was familiar with his master's predilections and catered to them with fawning servility, an obsequiousness calculated to yield later rewards.

John set about getting information about Devaki and accosted her when she was returning from picking flowers. He propositioned her, on his master's behalf, of course. Surely she'd seen that handsome young dorai who visited the temple the other day?

Indeed she had, and had been smitten. And she wasn't the only one, as she found when Kumara came to her as soon as Albert had left, expressing equally amorous thoughts, though in more explicit terms.

Nor, later, did it take much for Kumara to find out that Devaki was seeing the stranger.

- I know where you've been, Devaki. Don't look so surprised. It's a good thing no one else knows, otherwise you'll be thrown out of the temple. Your 'puravalar' won't like you giving away sex for free when he has to pay for it!
- I don't care. How can I tell you what I feel for this man, such desire, when I see his lovely white body ....
- Oh don't worry, I *also* feel the same when *I* imagine the virile youth! Actually no; he appears more like a wet fish, pink skin pouring with sweat ...
- Well, good thing you don't desire him, for *you* have

no chance with him, he only has eyes for *me*!

- Maybe I'll change my mind if you tell me more about that "glorious body" of his, so instead of talking about "your love" again, give me some juicy details about *his* body!
- Pō dā. You never take me seriously. But let me tell you Annan, I never imagined I could feel like this. I thought all unions would be the same as with 'puravalar': taken in lust, with no desire on my part, only disgust, indifference at best.
- Maybe 'puravalar' feels something for you … in his own way….
- No, I doubt he'll ever know the meaning of the word love, neither for god nor woman … not even for *you*!
- Yes, yes, mock me. You think you can afford to, now that you have "*found* true love; the *only* love". Like an awakened virgin! Silly silly girl; vellakāran are here today, gone tomorrow.
- I'm going to the 'valluvan' to make me a charm that will bind dorai to me, so that he can never leave me. I'll slip it under his mattress.
- Yennā iddah, what's this, luv-ve luv-ve? It's only because *you* feel differently about sex. Luv-ve is certainly not what that *vellakāran* feels! Oh, my little one, he is *no different* from 'puravalar', or any other men who might have you in future.

But Devaki was too smitten to catch Kumar's unusually serious undertone. She was sure the dorai reciprocated her feelings, for Albert had sent for her again, but it was only to alleviate his boring evenings. It was a strain to read by the smoky lamp, and worse to peruse files. Besides, his vanity was titillated by possessing one of "god's own", and it was sweet revenge to be dipping into that priest's pot of gold!

###

The inspection bungalow – better known as the TB (Travellers' Bungalow) – provided accommodation for officials touring muffasils. It was usually a plain building of standard PWD plan, though the ones in towns could be more than just basic: a living room flanked by two or four bedrooms with attached bathrooms. Bathrooms always had doors that opened onto the compound so that hot water was carried in to fill the tin tubs for baths, and the thunder-boxes could be cleaned out by the sweeper who could not enter any other rooms.

The living room extended back into a dining area, which gave way to the pantry. Food was brought from the kitchen, a detached unit, a little way off the main building. It was kept in a hot-case in the pantry, ready to be served. A veranda usually ran around at least the front of the building, deep and cool and open to what little breeze came in of an evening, which was where most guests spent their time.

Returning after an evening's shooting, servants rushed forward as Albert dismounted, to relieve him of his gun and hat. He threw himself on the easy chair. After his boots were taken off and the mud rubbed off his jodhpurs, he put his feet up on the chair's "long sleeves" extended for him. Soon John would be placing his chhota peg in the ring holder so conveniently attached to the chair arm. A common enough sight: the white raja enthroned on the veranda, ruling with cheroot as his sceptre and whisky glass for orb.

He was leaving early the next morning, so hadn't sent for the girl and resigned himself to an evening of solitude. He was therefore pleasantly surprised to see someone emerge from one of the rooms with maps rolled under his arm.

- Good heavens, another body in this godforsaken place?! I'm usually languishing on my own, pining for company. What a pity you didn't turn up earlier, I'm leaving tomorrow. I'm Albert Long. Are you here for *long*?
- Victor Poe, without any puns.
- I'm here to root out legal dirt. You?
- Digging out canals, a different kind of dirt I suppose.
- And you said "no puns"?! So what exactly ...?
- Oh, irrigation branch of the PWD. I'll probably be here a while. Some of these areas only have turloughs and we're looking to open up some irrigation canals. This is the only base for miles around. Thank goodness it's decent enough. And you?
- Looking into some irregularities, trying a few cases over land disputes ... alas, duty, duty. My first time

in this area, though I'll probably be back quite soon. The dignitary of my administration is the very devil for unnecessary bureaucratic detail and will want some cases followed up.

~ I hear Indians are a litigious lot, and devious? It was so odd: when I was riding to a possible site for a canal, a native ran alongside my horse and tried to press some coins into my hand, urgently appealing that the irrigation canal be brought nearer to his village.

~ Watch it: these indigenes are so cunning.

~ But we are allowed to accept phal-phool, fruits and flowers? I heard that those aren't considered bribes?

~ I think the native doesn't even think in terms of bribery. It's really a carry-over of their pagan practices: they offer their gods gifts, propitiating them when they want the grant of a favour, or as gratitude for fulfilment of their prayers. So they see us as authorities who have the *worldly power* to grant them what they want, so seek to appease *us* in the same way. They don't see it as something wrong, and are hurt when we refuse their offerings. Because we have the power to decide their fate – even if it's only in one aspect of their lives – they sees us as little gods. Just as well I suppose. It makes our jobs easier.

~ Though, from all I hear, deciding land cases is the most trying … or tempting or … what's the right word?

~ *Difficult.* They run circles around you unless you come down with a heavy hand. I just go with my instincts and quickly get the thing over with. Austin's

Jurisprudence not much good here! The native knows little and cares even less about legislation. They never understand, let alone appreciate, our methods of dealing with their affairs. Where's your drink?

- Sorry, I'm turning in early. Terrible indigestion; the worst thing about these tours is the awful food. In Madras, I'm in a chummery with an awful cook, so that doesn't let my stomach recover either. If my posting is confirmed, I'll find accommodation.
- Yes, you must try to have your Madras posting settled. Otherwise you might get stuck in an undesirable District, undermanned with only a native Magistrate, Assistant and Doctor. With "vairee little cul-cha thair, doncha knyeow"!

###

After Albert left, Victor didn't mind the solitude. In any case, he was usually too tired after his exhaustive surveys and turned in early, after his frugal dinner of soup and toast that suited his delicate stomach. His abstemiousness extended to liquor. He was glad he didn't drink; it was drink that made one crave fellowship, and vice versa. If there weren't drawings or notes to be made up of the day's work, he liked to read and was happy to turn in early with a good book – often even The Good Book.

When William Wilson arrived a few days later he was surprised to find someone reading on the veranda.

- I'm William Wilson. Well what er *luxury*! I usually find myself alone when I tour, though a centre as large as this usually does have one or two other occupants. Gosh it will be good to have some civilized conversation with someone over a drink. Though you …?
- No thanks. Don't drink. I'm Victor Poe. PWD Engineer.
- You here for a while?
- Looks like it. A lot of irrigation work is planned for this area. What brings you here?
- I'm with the ASI surveying er *temples*, though I also intend looking for some interesting dolmens and Jain caverns I hear are in this area.

William was not exactly reserved, but growing up in thrall to his mother's forceful personality, he came across as diffident and displayed characteristics typical of a middle child. When "er" jerked his conversation, he invariably emphasised the following word.

- This is my first tour. What on earth does one do in such a place?
- Yes, pretty unvarying. Breakfast, work, back for lunch at 1 – the er *intemperate* indulge in a pink gin before, read newspapers – last week's if you're lucky – and rest till 2.30. Then you might have interviews with people till 4. Your man will probably set up a table here on the veranda. After tea you could go shooting. Nothing very exciting here; mainly wild pig and small

game bird. Bath before drinks on the veranda. Dinner. Then attend to files again, if you're the er *conscientious* type.

- I suppose the lack of anything to do is not so different from some of the places my parents have been in.
- And they're …?
- Missionaries. Their missions have all been in the North and Central parts. And yours?
- My father's in er *trade*. He doesn't use the term but my mother did. In fact, she'd insist on putting it about that that was the reason they weren't er *admitted* to the er *Club*, just to see the controlled smirks on the ladies' faces! She thought it was hilarious. She didn't give a fig, she was so er *unconventional.*
- Was?
- Yes. She died when I was away at University. Oh, I do miss her. When I come upon some new find, I see it through her eyes. How she would have loved to discuss it with me! She knew so much about these things. What's more, she really er *loved* Indian culture.
- How did she meet your father then? They don't sound as if they had much in common. And she wouldn't have been in the Fishing Fleet surely?
- No, Mother certainly wasn't fishing for a husband. She came out because she'd heard about south Indian temples from a school teacher who'd been out here. She met my father in Madras and he proposed. She was glad to stay on, loved this country. Though she was appalled at the ingrown lives of the wives

living here, its er claustrophobic *triviality*. He had to promise her that she wouldn't be a merely decorative appendage, whose main asset was the ability to throw good dinner parties.

As my father has his own business, they could afford not "to fit in". No, she definitely didn't belong to the Club crowd, so not being members didn't affect her, as she had her lively mind and er *passionate* interests to sustain her.

- Oh, my parents never made it into a club either. Missionaries aren't considered 'prop-pah' Club material. Too down-at-heel-earnest for the likes of the pukka types.
- Right then. I'm off for a bath. See you later.

###

- Oh this blasted heat! I wish I could aestivate in some cool underground chamber till the rains come.
  Jo-hn, beer. I hope he's kept some on ice.
- Oh you're back, Albert? And you'll soon see William Wilson from ASI.
- Full house eh? Just what I need, civilized company after trying blasted cases. Lord, can they go on for ages, damn litigious natives! Sitting in that stuffy room that passes for a magistrate's court, trying to unravel convoluted land disputes. That languid punka. I wish it could shoo away the press of litigants, but it barely manages to move flies!

Ah, and who have we here? So you're the ASI chap? We'll soon be able to set up a rubber of whist at this rate! Right-o, see you both at dinner.

It was an embarrassment when they met in the dining room. The table was properly laid out with white damask and silverware and even a bowl of flowers, John's efforts at making a tour feel like home for his master. Though he managed to suppress all other signs of disapproval, Albert's nostrils flared on seeing Victor, who found he'd been caught short sartorially:

- Albert, you're *dressed* for dinner, out here in the sticks?
- Ye-es Victor, have to maintain prestige in front of the natives, *wherever* we are. They *expect* it. They'd lose respect for us if we didn't.
- Well I'm sorry, I didn't think I'd need the formality on tour. And I don't remember my parents changing for dinner, when I used to come home from school.

Albert went all sniffy and thought, "Well, what do you expect from missionaries; some of them have gone half-native anyway". Instead, he said aloud:

- Well, I've only honoured you with dinner jacket and black tie. In town, I'd be wearing the works.
- In that Madras er *heat*? My mother always said we are so impractical, not adapting to local conditions. You know, those John Company white nabobs wore native dress. Why, so did Francis Ellis, er *Collector* of Madras no less, and that was as recently as 1810. Wonderful

man that. He's the one that set up the college of Fort St George; the man who taught us Tamil was from that institution.

- Huh, all very well William, but that was *before* the Mutiny, before we took over. Now we can't let the side down.

William decided to change the subject before things got even more awkward.

- Mmmm … these mangoes are delicious.
- Yes, they're the one consolation in this blasted hot season. Not bad for local ones. The ones you get around Bombay are the best. Alphonsos, as those Portuguese named them, blasted cheeky fellas!
- First time I'm eating mangoes. I'd heard so much about them from my father's Anglo-Indian uncle, who dreams about them in his retirement in Cheltenham.
- They are even better when you eat them the way I did as a child: er *strip* down to nothing but underpants, tear the skin away with your teeth and bite into the flesh, trying to catch with your tongue the juice that trickles down your hands. Quite an art that! Then after I'd eaten all the pulp, I liked sucking the seed till the fibre was dry and stiff. It always reminded me of the phrase I'd read in books: "so scared, his hair stood on end". The mango seed was like an er *illustration* of that! Then ayah would sluice me down with a bucket of cold water and rub me down in the sun.

Yes, the mango: it's a completely different eating

experience when you eat it with your hands and more than one of your er *senses* is involved.

- Huh, none of *that* here, thenk-kyoo. Peeled and cut in neat little cubes to be forked up, the polite way to eat at table.

  And John knows it, thank goodness. He's as keen as his master to keep the flag flying, and has appointed himself chief flagstaff! Well, bed for me. Early start tomorrow.

###

Kumara's warning proved true. Albert was gone, after Devaki had visited him three times. She was inconsolable, despite all Kumara's efforts at teasing her out of it.

Even the Priest noticed:

- Annan, Guruggal wants to see me. Amma says he's not happy with my dancing. And do you think he … he *knows* … you know, about *that* …? Please come with me, you must.

###

- What's the matter with you Devaki? You can't even remember your mudras, your nritta couldn't keep up with the tālam …. Need I remind you yet again of your role? You're not a raja-dasi, dancing for some princeling's entertainment. When a deva-dasi dances, even when no one is watching her, her own soul has to be satisfied because her dance is an offering to God.

- But she's been practising a lot, Guruggal.
- Be quiet Kumara, I want to hear from her, rather than from her spokesman. So Devaki, it must be *something else* troubling you then? Are you perhaps seeking satisfaction where it can't be found? Your main duty is to God and God alone, and that should give you all the pleasure and satisfaction you seek.

  Come on Devaki, tears are no answer.

The emotional or erotic imperative dismisses the stability of devotional union, though in bharathnatyam such awareness is meant to be retained even in the unison. Dance repeats the movements of the planets and stars, mudras symbolise the doing of the gods, full of meaning and purport.

Bharathnatyam's symbolic gestures are not universal. How could they be, particularly in those insular days? But those who had the religious frame of reference, understood them. Its mime – for the mere narration of a story – has perhaps always been more readily understood by all, but only the cognoscenti can read its more esoteric alphabet.

However, one can admire the body as pure movement and grace, like an abstract painting, without looking for meaning. Equally, one can be titillated and aroused by the body's sensuality, or transported by its divine significance.

- Which other profession besides yours embraces the polarities of bodily satiation and ascetic discipline: profanation and sanctity, from the depths of degradation to an enforcement of order and the purest love; encompassing naraka and swarga, nadir and zenith?

Bharathnatyam speaks for all those who have been deprived of voices: your body gives a tongue, your hands make them speak, gives eloquence to those inarticulate emotions – desire, longing, hate, rage – all the underground feelings one can't communicate, thoughts one can't elaborate. When one cannot raise one's own voice, dance takes us to that harmonic rapture, establishing a heaven on earth with musical initiative and your body.

When you can do so much, what *else* is it you desire? Tears won't wash away whatever it is .... This restlessness in you ... could it be a stirring caused by your dance? After a spinning nritta, haven't you felt some rare bliss surfacing inside you like froth, like the nectar of immortality yielded up during samudra manthan, when the ocean was churned? The spinning, the spinning, it's all in the spinning.

As Sufi dervishes know.

– Nataraja in the dark void, briefly illuminated by his circlet of flames that spins, never consuming itself. His drum beats out the fourteen syllables that form the basis of language. He spins Creation into being, his locks flying ... some great centrifugal force whose centre remains still and self-contained.

> He watches what he has thrown out, how it moves beyond his control: the energy ripples find their own way, to determine their own journey through time and space. Equipoise after all the hurly burly.
> Have you not felt within yourself that glory of creation? That *power*, not egotistical or despotic or cruel, that spins the Self out of existence, till you know not who or what you are, and feel only beautiful pure *energy*?

The Priest absently picked up fistfuls of raw rice, from the platter in front of him and let grains run through his fingers.

- After that primal separation, there can only be yearning, yearning for that eternal reunion.

He summarily dismissed them, almost unaware of their presence, as if he was embarrassed at having said too much, or that the shadow of mortality had suddenly obscured the present.

###

Work kept the three Englishmen in the area for several days and, despite differences in outlook and opinions, they looked forward to each other's company at day's end. One evening while having their drinks on the veranda – Albert had not been able to persuade Victor to abandon his lime juice for even a beer, let alone the customary whisky – they saw a native girl being taken round the back by John.

- Looks like you don't need us for your evening's er *entertainment*, Albert ...? Was that your er *visitor* sneaking in just now ...?
- Oh, is she here already? Blast, why is she so early? I rather think she fancies me, silly wench. After notes are written up, not much to do here after sunset and I was alone, so I've sent for her a few times.

  Anyway, I'm off soon, so just a temporary convenience. She's the nautch girl at a temple not far from here. Yes Victor old boy, you've actually seen a nautch girl! Don't look so shocked. Ha ha ha, I'm not being bribed, though she's phal-phool alright: *delicious*, though I wish she could be more *fragrant*. Phew, sometimes all her bodily fluids stink! Don't know what that very pungent spice is, but it's *disgusting*. I could smell it in her every pore and orifice! I nearly sent her away the other day but then she satisfied me by servicing me with the least physical contact, if you get my meaning? One of the Cammersootra tricks no doubt!

William interjected, to save Victor being subjected to further detail:

- Probably 'vendiam', er *fenugreek*. They eat the leaves and seeds as it's supposed to be good for one's blood sugar and ....
- Ha ha, reek of fenugreek, eh?
- Albert I'm shocked that you're *encouraging* the pernicious

practice of temple prostitutes when you're supposed to ….

- Natives see nothing obscene in it, Victor. Whatever is offered God inevitably ends up for the benefit of venal mortals.
- Like you? We missionaries have been trying to stamp out temple prostitution for years and thank goodness it looks like our government is succeeding. And the good thing is that some of the natives have also seen the iniquity of the system and have joined the eradication campaign.

  So what kind of an example are you …?
- I don't give a toss whether or not temples have their girls! What I can't understand is our higher-ups closing down comparatively safe approved soldiers' brothels, claiming clap's so rampant. So naturally our men were driven to street women, so it increased rather than decreased. Doncha know, mining for Gold and Silver to present to their wives!
- Er, I don't think Victor quite catches your drift …
- Gonorrhoea and Syphilis man! Ha ha, Victor Poe, Po-face but not poker by nature!

  Anyway, so not only was there an increase in those "precious metals" but worse was what went on in the barracks between the men. Can you imagine what homosexuality does to discipline – the domination, blackmail, insubordination? Well, what do they expect those poor devils to do without sex? So now the higher-ups look the other way if it's a clean girl willing to give us her services. Yes, I've had a few of them, particularly during my tours. Doncha know, in the line of duty!

- Sounds more like a er *bonus* to me!
- We-ell I'm quite willing to share my good fortune: my John can fix the both of you up with native wenches here. You'll soon get a taste for playing on the browns.
- Funny you should use the expression "playing". It's the same word in Tamil for er *philandering*. And does your predilection for er *native women* have anything to do with your having been very attached to the ayah who brought you up …?
- *Wha-at??* My ayah as an object of sexual desire! She was a crone, who wore no blouse under her sari so one glimpsed her breasts. We boys got such a thrill seeing them and we'd purposely throw things down, so that she'd have to bend down to pick them up, and we'd get a glimpse of her breasts, though we disguised our prurience by giggling. In hindsight, I can't think why we were fascinated: they were like shrivelled up mangoes! She had pawned off her earrings, so her distended earlobes swung almost as much as her breasts ….
- Oh yes 'kātolai', it's the rolled palm leaf they use to er *widen* their earlobes. You obviously didn't recognise one of their signs of beauty, Albert!
- Thenk-kyoo, Professor Wilson; most interesting blasted dissertation! And add these further signs of her beauty to your notes: her teeth stuck out like a coconut-scraper and her mouth was stained with

betel nut …. My ayah certainly has nothing to do with my "playing on the browns"! It's just down to supply and demand; I take what I can get. Only in the big cities do you get the country-breds. Or even our own girls who have let the side down by making themselves available.

- Country-breds?
- Four annas in the rupee … chow anni. You must have heard that expression up north, Victor?
- My mother has very strong views on such ... what she calls *miscegenation*. Won't even have a female servant working in the house: sends them all to the mission school and hospital.
- Yes, strange how racial mixtures everywhere are detested. Hindus call it 'samkara', their main concern with miscegenation being with er *caste* pollution, 'varna-samkara'.
- There you go, Professor Wilson's Tamil lesson for the day. It's called putting out olive branches, doncha know Professor Wilson? And laughable how some of them claim "Spanish descent", in wishing away their tincture!
- Thenk-kyoo, Professor Long, for your er *short* dissertation! And since you have left your instruction in my hands, I have to point out that 'varna-samkara' is *Sanskrit*, not Tamil.

As I was saying, looking askance at mixed races the world over is perhaps not so strange: they're usually the result of 'mésalliance', white men er *raping* or taking advantage of the native female.

I can well understand your mother's feelings, Victor. Half-breed children are uncomfortable reminders of that unbridled lust the white man has displayed; that old Adam, that animal we want to keep caged and hidden.

- Well, you're doing a good job of that, Victor, keeping your animal well-caged and hidden! You still haven't escaped your missionary upbringing. Haven't had a native lass yet, then? I'll have to get my John to rectify that! Get you one who knows some Cammersootra tricks, like my minx does!
- Stop picking on him Alfred. That girl, from the glimpse I had of her, she doesn't look completely er *Indian* …?
- Yes, I agree William; she's a bit fairer than most I've seen around here. Aren't they Dravidian, very dark and rather aboriginal?
- Fishing for a closer look are you, you devil Victor!
- Most certainly not! Really Alfred, you're impossible. And aren't you worried about ... well ... the um "metals" you just mentioned?
- Pō-pō, as the Tamils would say: ha ha isn't that a good pun, Victor Pō-pō?! You really are new to this country, aren't you! No-o Victor, you're alright if you protect yourself with the Cardinal C's: Carbolic, Caustic, Condys solution and Chlorine water.

- I could add another er *prophylactic C*, though it might not suit you, Albert: *Chastity*!
- It certainly wouldn't, William, though no doubt it's first on Victor's list!

  So-o, I'm off: wench is waiting for me with open arms – and legs – and I don't care how many annas in the rupee!

10

~ Why are you drinking so much water Devaki? There won't be enough left for the evening meal so it's your turn to go to the well and fetch more. I filled the pot this morning.

~ I have to flush this smell out of my system. Annan, tell me: do I stink of 'vendiam'?

~ Oh, so lover boy smelled it on you, did he?

~ Yes, I almost died of shame when he made a face and told me to go away.

~ Why didn't you just tell him he smells like a pig?

~ Only you can talk like that … that too, you wouldn't dare say it to *him*.

~ Come closer, let me smell you. Do you smell it on me? Since we've both eaten it, we can't smell it on each other. But I know one's urine stinks of it and you can smell the place where one has urinated, even when you're just passing by.

- I'm not going to eat it again, though I really like the dish Amma makes with it.
- It's good for you. Purifies the blood, like bitter gourd. Now there's something I hate the taste of.

###

Albert departed the next day. Devaki knew of his comings and goings only when she was sent for by him. If a few days went by without a summons, Devaki was wracked not only by separation, but by not knowing whether he would be back. She felt a visceral desolation at the thought that she would never see him again. The anguish stirred a memory in her.

She had been asked to dance at her patron's house for some guests the family wanted to impress. After the assignment, she'd just left the house, when her sari caught in her anklet. She bent down to release it and happened to glance back when she straightened up. She saw puravalar's young wife, who still bore signs of a new bride, peeping through the barred window of the living room women normally didn't enter. It looked out onto the street, so the wife and Devaki saw each other for the first time and Devaki was taken aback by her expression, though she didn't give it much thought then.

The wife's face now came into clear focus; it was a look

of appraisal, but underlying it was something else which Devaki couldn't fathom at the time. She now understood that gaze: it was wounded incomprehension, of having to share her husband, her beloved godling around whom her life revolved. So that's what his wife felt, the torment of love and pain Devaki felt each time she left Albert, the separation of love and longing so eloquently described by poets ... no date set for his return, the jealousy of imagining him with another woman.

###

However, William did not disguise his relief at Albert's departure.

- Thank goodness he's gone. I couldn't take much more of his drawling cynicism and the arch way he looks to see if we're sufficiently impressed by his "clever" remarks.

  Smug bod, sniffing in such a supercilious way when our views don't tally with his!
- Quite the popular bachelor around town it appears. He was telling me what an active social life he has: the Races, dancing attendance on the ladies at balls, burra khanas, regular at the club bar ....
- Well, it's a good thing he's so er *ambitious* so can't afford to neglect his work, though he probably holds court on his veranda after his early morning ride, gazette in one hand and his coffee in the other, supposedly listening to daily reports and complaints,

but his mind doubtless on the girl he's booked the first dance with, or which horse to bet on in the afternoon Races .... There must be some like er *him* in your chummery?

~ Only one fortunately, and he's also too busy swanning around for us to meet that often! I thought about moving into a house, but I don't like housekeeping. And I don't think I could treat servants the way the Service expects us to. My parents' household was quite different.

~ Yes, all those notions precious to the likes of Albert: "waving the red, white and blue ... not letting the side down". Thank goodness my mother enabled us to be free of all that. Oh, I had a happy childhood.

~ So did I. Four sisters and a brother, so we had each other for company, and we were also allowed to play with servants' children and those who worked in the Mission. All converts, so they were "natives", but we just didn't think of them in that way.

~ Yes, we fraternised with servants' children too, much to the disapproval of our neighbours. It was funny actually, for I used to see their boy and little girl with the mali's son, but Anthony was such a bully, bent upon asserting his superiority. Elaine was a great friend of my sister's. They were allowed to come around whenever their mother wanted to er *waltz* off somewhere, though the father didn't approve of us at all. And then Edward and I were sent away to school, much against my mother's wishes.

– Yes mine too. My father's mission was sending him to India. I know it broke my mother's heart to leave me behind but the Mission was paying for our schooling in England. Just us boys, not the girls, lucky them. I know my parents wanted to take me to India but they knew I would have to be sent back after a couple of years for mainstream schooling, and they doubted the Mission would pay for that extra trip.

I barely knew how to wipe my bottom when my parents left me. My brother was too young. He joined me two years later. I boarded with a missionary family. There were five other boys whose parents worked in missions in China and Africa. That was quite interesting actually; we'd tell each other about "our" countries and exchange stamps.

We had to attend church regularly but I didn't mind as I loved singing in the choir. My years there inculcated in me a passionate love for music. I still join a choir wherever I can, and listen to choral music records. After a day of hearing people's inanities, harangues or gripes, I like to be reminded that the human voice is capable of such beauty.

In Nagpur there was an 8-year-old girl in the choir whose voice was so pure that I felt the heavens open. She seemed to let a pristine gentle white light through, with that angelic quality of her voice.

– Goodness, my experience is so very different from yours! When I hear the organ play in church, I feel there's something so very ominous. I imagine a wrathful god parting the clouds and thrusting down a punitive hand … a very Blakean image ....

- Didn't mind church so much as the food. Those Guardians of the Flock seemed to feel our main source of nourishment should be the Scriptures, so the stomach didn't count for much: the food was really grim! Dripping on bread was the worst. That awful smell and the claggy texture of cold grease that stayed on the tongue! We would have been happier having just plain bread.
- The dish I hated most was sago porridge. Frog's spawn we called it. I didn't know whether it was better to chew or just swallow that slimy mess. In our vivid imaginations we thought of them turning into er *tadpoles* wriggling in our stomachs so that made us reluctant to chew! Chew or swallow, it was such a difficult decision!
- And lumpy porridge gone cold, awful ... Funny thing is, porridge is a bunger-up! In England we boys were always *constipated* in any case, so why they chose to give us further "binders", I'll never know. Cheap I suppose.

  Ooh, when I came to this country, it was just the opposite, couldn't stop the "runs" with all the curry!
- Can't say I had that problem. I suppose I grew up eating curry. But it certainly did make me even more er *constipated* in boarding school, without any spice.
- Curry, so where does that word come from, William?
- Well, it might be from the Tamil word 'karivéppilai',

the curry leaves which they use in almost all their dishes. But it's also said that when Vasco da Gama wanted to take over Calicut, he mutilated the captured Muslim seamen and sent parts to the Zamorin to make 'karil' out of them.

- I thought years of that bland stodge in England would cure me of the effects of the amoebic dysentery I caught here as a child. But no, it can still play havoc with my digestive system. That's why I don't drink. Though, of course, Albert puts it down to my "puritanism".
- Good heavens Victor, you can't let yourself be judged by the likes of a libertine like Albert! It irks him that his opinion of me doesn't affect me in the least. In fact, he knows that I scorn him for his er *louche* attitudes and values. And oddly enough, my opinion of him *does* seem to bother him.
- Well, my parents hardly drank either. Though in their case it was paucity of funds as well as moral rectitude that prevented them from joining the Club, that is, if they were deemed admissible in the first place! But as you know, my post makes it mandatory to join the club but, even now that I've "got in", I find I can do without "going to the Club". And I was happy to be able to tell my parents that they haven't missed much! How I detested those years away from home! On Sundays we weren't allowed to do anything besides read the Good Book.

In fact, I was taught to read exclusively on Sunday

school literature. And, as for playing with our toys or any indoor games, that was out of the question. Oh, they were kind in a Christian way, but sharp on discipline.

~ Yes, I suppose that's also what makes Albert so different: when he was sent to England for schooling, he lived with his grandparents and was quite spoiled by the looks of it.

~ I went on to boarding school when I was six. My brother joined me a year later and having to look out for him was an added distress. Poor frightened little chappie used to wet his bed.

More cold hardship in those metal beds and almost frozen mattresses, ice-cold water washes at six in the morning; playing games in all weathers, in shorts. And starched matrons didn't exactly qualify as creature comforts, the way ayahs did.

~ Thank goodness I wasn't too young when I was sent off, but it was bad enough after a home life in India. I almost lost touch with my Tamil but picked it up at university. I grew up hearing Tamil, so it made sense to study the language, as I knew that counting backwards in er *Persian* wasn't going to be of any use to me! And taking the exam ups one's salary immediately. More chances of promotion as well.

~ I suppose I can find a good teacher of Tamil in these parts? I'm handicapped because I have to rely on an interpreter. I need one for some basics like taking measurements and things, so I thought I'd learn the language. But Tamil limits one to this Presidency, doesn't it, not much scope for forging ahead here?

- Tamil's not even good in er *all* parts of this Presidency, only in its south eastern reaches. Fortunately, there's enough of archaeological interest in this area to keep me busy for a lifetime. And I like this part of the country, the south.
- Yes, people here seem so much gentler, something more vulnerable about them, though they are so exasperating sometimes. And venality seems to be a common denominator.

  But they are different from people up north … can't put my finger on it.
- They're less aggressive perhaps. And I think the southerner's loyalty and love is genuine.
- Well, I imagine good ones are good ones anywhere. I've seen many in my sojourns up north.
- Racially, too, northerners are so different. Which reminds me … er *"Albert's girl"*, unusual beauty, not typically south Indian ...
- Sounds like you wouldn't mind a go with her ...?
- Well, wouldn't you ...?
- Definitely not! She's an example of the institution we're trying to abolish! But ye-es, if we're talking about women in general .... It's odd, though my parents never openly discussed sex with us, they managed to instil very definite strictures about it.

  When we boys were on holiday from school, my mother made us take cold baths. I'm sure she believed it would dampen any sexual desires.

- I think she'd be surprised that that er *notion* has something in common with a Hindu belief: that a woman's water can quench or dilute sexual fire. So I suppose cold showers aren't so far of the mark!

Victor, whose nineteenth century evangelical upbringing had effectively blocked any regard for Indian art and culture, having heard often enough from his parents that Hinduism was the worst kind of heathenism, admired William for retaining his youthful knowledge and admiration for India, for holding fast to his views, despite exposure to other values; influential intellectuals at university perhaps, or peer pressure .... Of course, his mother probably played a large part in William's enduring love for what he regarded as his cultural home.

- Trouble is, I have been brought up to believe that to be with a woman ....
- You mean have er *carnal* relations with one?
- Yes, that it should always be accompanied by love and companionship. Which is impossible if I couldn't *communicate* with a native. You know Tamil, so *you* could with this girl.

Victor had noticed that William's conversation often reverted to Albert and "his girl" so Victor's last remarks were in the hope that William would be more forthcoming about his feelings for "Albert's girl". Though Victor had correctly detected an element of "methinks

William doth protest too much", he was too naïve to realise it was William's *jealousy* of Albert, specifically of Albert's alacrity in using native women so easily and without compunction.

Victor's perception wasn't far off the mark: William was attracted to "Albert's girl", but that appeal extended to Indian women generally. Having grown up to see them as more than mere functionaries, he liked their gentleness, admired their limpid beauty. And when they weren't being subservient or trying to ape their masters, their culture came through, giving them integrity and dignity.

But, for all his liberal background, William didn't have the courage to bed an Indian girl. Or it could have been some confusion in his attitude: what sort of equivalence would there be in such a sexual encounter? And he certainly didn't have – or wish to have – Albert's callous disregard of the native that enabled him to treat them as expendables. Nonetheless, his inability to do what Albert did so easily, resulted in a mocking criticism of him that subconsciously sought to disguise his envy, something that Victor correctly sensed.

###

One evening, when Victor returned from work, a middle-aged Indian was waiting under the tamarind tree. William emerged from his bedroom.

– Oh no, I thought I gave my clerk strict instructions

that none of these petitioners was to come here.

– No, no, Victor, this one is here to see me. What is it Ramasami?

Ramasami sidled onto the veranda.

– Ah, you've brought the album.

– What's that then: illustrations of the Cammersootra?

– Well Victor, come and have a dekko. Let's forget your religious upbringing and give you some views in matters of the flesh!

– You jest; but it is probably *because* of my background that I am so confused. Sometimes I get so fed up of all that god-bothering that I try turning away from it. But then I feel guilty. I suppose there is a via media but I need to find it for myself.

– Well Victor, goodness knows one *needs* a strong ethical code, if not religion, in this country. No, I was teasing. The subject matter of this album is more mundane.

Right, Ramasami. I'll look through the album. I'll let you know if I want to buy it. And you'll have those plans you sketched today, drawn up tomorrow? Yes, good night.

– Oh I say, these paintings are rather fine! Done by that chap?

– No, Ramasami's the one who sketches the temples, their plans and sculptural detail. Lives in a village fairly close by, a family of artists. His father did these paintings for a lady in Madras, but they weren't finished before she left. Sadly typical; time means nothing to these people, so he's rather stuck with them. Looking to sell them.

- Pity. I would've definitely taken them if they were illustrations of the Cammersootra!

William chuckled, appreciating Victor's rare show of humour against himself.

- What vivid colours. Interesting the way he's attempted perspective.
- And yet he hasn't quite got it right. Indian artists were employed in the royal courts and did portraits and commissions. But they were flat and one dimensional, without any shading.

  When that patronage dwindled, they turned to doing postcards and albums of monuments and places of scenic interest, for the memsahibs who wanted to give an idea of their life here to those back Home. These artists had to adapt their technique to satisfy western norms by adding perspective, shading …
- They're almost shiny, viewed from some angles …
- That's an attempt to imitate paintings on glass, which were popular in Europe. These are on mica, which is found widely throughout this area. Could get brittle with time.

  This set is quite unusual, showing occupations of this region. The best Company Paintings I've seen were in Vellore, chap called Yellapah. Most "sets" were done in north India, where the Mughal Imperial style of painting was strong. Sets like these went out of fashion when India was no longer "the exotic East" to those at Home. This Madras doraisani must have wanted one of South Indian occupations.

###

- Are you mad Devaki? You're going to that vellakāran almost every day. Do you think I haven't seen that snake Ja-ahn sneaking around to conduct you to his master's summons? I have *told* you what will happen to you if you get caught.
- It's all right now, because I've told Amma I've got my periods, so I am staying in the outhouse and no one will notice when I come and go. Amma would have, but little chance of getting caught by her since she's not well and not moving around much. But that excuse will only give me a few days more.
  You must help me after that. And yes, I *am* mad: mad for him! He's even removed all my clothes to see my naked body!
- As if I'm interested in *your* body, Devaki. Tell me, tell me what *he's* like naked! Do these vella-kāran, white-men, also have 'vella' cocks? I believe their heads down there are red, like their faces in the sun ...?
- Chee, stop that kind of talk! I won't tell you anything if you say such things.
- Oh, I thought that since you've discovered the joys of sex you would like to talk about such things.

- Oh be quiet, you … what I've found is beautiful, not the sex you talk about. And yes, he *is* beautiful, *all over*. Oh, even when I first saw him, how I wanted his body! Desire yes, but so much more than just desire. His body is only part of what I feel for him.

  I felt *one* with him; it isn't just obsequious worship like it is when I serve god. It is the same kind of overwhelming emotion I've been told I *should* feel when I dance: an obliterating oneness with the object of one's devotion. I've never felt it. But now I have, with a mere mortal, even in our moments of sheer lust.

  Except that it is more than lust; it is *love* I feel for him. Even if he only feels lust for me, it is so different from the lust I've had thrust on me by 'puruvalar'. Annan, I feel sorry for you, that you haven't known such feelings.
- Ayyō ayyō ayyō, how can I make you *see sense* Devaki? I've told you, you are nothing but a desirable *convenience* to him only as long as he's here.

Kumara did not know the term "typical Victorian hypocrite", otherwise he might have added: the white man comes here to ban our forbidden fruit, and then walks off with the pick of the basket, to feast on surreptitiously. As if, like the mango, the yielding flesh's undisguised deliciousness was best enjoyed in private.

###

A couple of months passed before William found

himself alone in the TB. He heard that Victor had been there earlier but was away surveying for a couple of days, though William was also going off to find Jain caverns some distance away. He'd have to camp, but Muthu was used to getting everything ready for life under canvas in the hardiest of terrain.

However, someone else turned up before he left:

- *You* here again Albert? I thought you'd finished your er *work* in this area?
- Been back a few times actually, chasing up matters for my "Conscientious Superior".
- Getting inky fingers?
- Yes, my blasted Joint Magistrate's drowning in his ink well. He's hoping to curry favour with the Judge with all this excess of bureaucratic detail, hoping to court the Judge's niece who's just come out. But little does he know I'm a step ahead of him. *I've* already filled her dance card at the Ball the Judge is giving for her!

  Oh, these punctilious functionaries … my Joint wants *full* reports on revenues settlements, remissions, land tax … Bad enough adjudicating minor wickedness and crime in town: cases involving pecuniary disputes, the milliner's unpaid bill, or some spiv being dunned by his creditors ... Christ, it never ends!

  Jo-ohn, cold beer! What, you the only one here? I'd thought there'd be a brace in the bag. Where's that other chap, Poe? Name suits him: talk about poker-face! Though it looks like he has it up the other end!
- Oh, it's hardly surprising his background's made him

rather er *rigid*.

- *Rigid*? Po po, I *hardly* think so! Alright, alright, no need to groan; my puns aren't that bad. But good thing Victor isn't here, for here's my evening's entertainment. No grass under John's feet! He must have sent for her immediately.

###

Despite Kumara's misgivings, this summons gave Devaki false hope yet again, for Albert's love-making seemed particularly ardent. He fingered with morbid fascination the raised flesh made by the mark of Shiva burned into her thigh. Branded her as the Lord's? Well, he would show their Lord that even a mortal, an "unclean foreigner" like him, could take what was His!

- I'm your new god then, eh? Come, worship me again. Do all your lovely heathen poo-jaas and libations to my ling-gum. Anoint me, wench. I have a Christian heart but my vital parts are most decidedly pagan! Blast ... you don't understand a word of what I'm saying; just as well. Lord, what am I getting myself into?

###

Victor had also returned to the TB, having toured the further reaches of the area. He and William wondered what Albert was getting into, when he waxed rather lyrical about the native girl, for he was also boasting that his courtship of the Judge's niece in Madras was going well.

- Laetitia's come out on connubial spec and the Judge's wife has given me to understand that she's backing *my bid* as suitor!
- Then I can't understand why you are still seeing that temple girl. Haven't you been reprimanded about such behaviour?
- You're not going to sneak on me, are you Victor? Just maintain that po-face when you meet my betters in church! *Joke,* Victor! They aren't likely to find out what goes on in this backwater. Even if John does gossip with other servants, as long as the Judge's wife doesn't get wind of it … But there's something different about this girl. She's so direct in the way she comes here and offers herself to me, a desire so unselfconscious it opens her body as smoothly as a sari sliding off. Very different from cutting a swathe through sartorial bulwark to reach the fountainhead of our virgins!
- Well, that's all part of er *her job*, surely?
- And yet she has more *mystery* than any of her simpering colleagues or other coy professionals.
- *Mystery*? (Winking at William) That's probably because she doesn't say a word to you, Albert, knowing you don't speak her language!
- Ho ho, oh Po, your attempts at humour are pathetic! Wait, I know what it is: she's *straight,* that's why she's different. Everyone else in this blasted country is so

serpentine. Never being direct, even the vegetation twines and clings and obscures ... creepers and tendrils ... She by-passes all those slithering coils ...

- Looks like you're getting caught in er *her coils*, Albert! (Winking at Victor) From all you've just said about her, it sounds a lot like love to me!
- Yes, watch it: you're getting in deeper than the Judge's niece would like you to!
- Nonsense, I probably got carried away only because she's so different from her kind.
- No-oo, it looks a lot like she's more than just a er *temporary* arrangement!
- Not for me it isn't. If she thinks she loves me, then more fool she; no future for her with me. I wouldn't give up my position, the society of my fellow countrymen, my way of life for ... for what? I'm getting all she can give me, in any case.
- Unless you dread the day you can have no more of it?
- Oh, there'll always be others will give it me; though I grant you, perhaps not with all her *skills*. No, it's going to be a *wife* for me: a well-bred English girl who'll share my life.

However, Albert silently admitted to himself that the sensuous hedonism in the abandoned parting of this girl's pantaloons would not be duplicated in the dismantling of the starchy uprightness of an English wife's whalebone and hoops. But he weighed in with more important compensations.

~ As I told you, the girl I have in my sights, Laetitia, will even advance my career.

~ You sly dog! You've really got yourself set up, haven't you?

~ As long as whatever happens here, stays here. Everyone does it, so I'm not exactly a marked man. Our women know it. It's unspoken, tacit. What do they expect us to do, when they go to the hills or Home for months on end? And I suspect our good Judge himself is not above a little something on the side! He has nautch-debauch at some of his dinners. Tries to pass it off as part of his duty, "the important local gentry – zamindars, petty rajas – *expect* it as part of my hospitality, doncha know". As if the old geezer doesn't enjoy it! However, if my Joint heard about this little affair, being my rival for the attentions of Laetitia, he'd sink my chances.

Anyway, I think I'm a good nose ahead of that dried up beanpole. D'you know, he's even been turned down by the spins! Yes, I think it's safe to say I can look forward to being Magistrate before long, once I marry Laetitia.

~ So what's she like?

~ She's quite good on the piano, and not a bad voice either … unfortunately, all gums when she laughs … nice clewed-in waist though.

[Clew, another link to my favourite word: it's the thread – it can also be the ball of thread – that can guide one through a labyrinth. Hence the word clue, that which helps you solve a mystery].

Victor had listened to the conversation in uncomfortable silence:

- And what about you William? No Commissioner's daughter in your sights?
- I'm not in town often. Visiting out of the way sites takes up a lot of my time. And I don't er *socialise* that much when I am. My mother wasn't a club person, so my father and I don't go either.
- Don't you think your father might be glad to be rid of that particular injunction of your mother's? Perhaps he sneaks off to the club when you're not home, relieved to go back to the fold of the bar, glad to be boxed in with the boxwallahs?
- I doubt it, Albert. And are boxwallahs now admitted to the club? I'm so out of touch. When I'm home, my father and I enjoy being with each other. My mother really left such a hole in our lives, which is why he's er *nudging* me towards matrimony. Feels the house could do with the feminine touch again.
- Hah, William the Conqueror, hasn't vanquished the Fishing Fleet yet?
- I doubt the Fishing Fleet would float a good catch my way, Albert. Or rather, a er *suitable* one. I find that those girls come out with a rather rosy view of the life they expect to lead here and I'm not sure they could adjust. I suppose I'm really looking for someone ...

- … like your mother?!
- Well ye-es, someone who already knows something about this country and has accepted its ways. I can't expect a wife to love it the way my mother did, but I'd like a girl to have at least some familiarity with it.
- Your turn, Victor.
- I don't know. I can't get married just yet in any case. But I agree with William: there's much to be said for a wife from a similar background. I see what sacrifices my mother's made to support my father, to further the mission in which they both have so much faith.

  Goodness, they've been in some really appalling outposts. That concept of self-sacrifice ... of course, you see it here with all the native women, how they treat their husbands as gods. Well, I wouldn't expect my wife to, heh heh, *blaspheme* in that way, nor do I go that far in my needs of a wife, but I do feel that a girl who has seen her parents' sacrifice in awful conditions, is more likely to make the same adjustments.

  Not that I think my postings will have the same grim demands and disadvantages.
- So she'll probably be from a missionary family?
- That would be ideal.
- You have to watch that abstinent Christian spirituality, Victor! The hair-shirt doubles as a Girdle of Venus! Anything that is a constant irksome reminder of a sinful Fall, is but a clinging invitation to fall further!
- Albert, besides being an appalling metaphor-mixer,

are you sure you're not a secret er *Tantric*? They have this curious notion that if you fall far enough into the bottomless pit of sin, you'll fall all the way through, to heavenly eternity!

[SD: If William was our contemporary, he would have called it a Black Hole that sucks you in and throws you out on the other side. And he could have added: like the China Syndrome, tunnelling through to find yourself in America – though that's not everyone's idea of paradise!]

- Me, one of those naked *fakeers*? Aren't Tantrics the ones who indulge in human sacrifice? We're trying to stamp them out. We Jacks in Office have a hard enough time here without getting caught up in such vile practices.

  And that's why the proverbial good woman behind every successful man is so important: in my case, to advance my career, consolidate my position and hold up the social end.

  Though it's shocking that officials like us are expected to be available at all hours to appellants. Interrupts one's social life no end!
- Our officials here are very much masters of those they govern. The norm back Home is the other way around: the official's job is to er *serve* the people.
- Really William, can you see one of our officials at Home entertaining a petition when he's at the pub?

- I agree with William. I pity the common man here: a supplicant to all officialdom, even to any of his fellow-countrymen who wields any administrative power, from judge to *chaprasi.*

  But William, you're lucky in that I imagine you're not in the line of all officialdom's hazards: petitions, bribes ...
- Yes Victor, fortunately little of that. I agree with you that official machinery will grind the common man down to sycophantic appeal and, failing that, to rampant er *bribery* – all of which has stopped the officer's ears to any compassionate appeal.
- Oh, you innocents, you both have obviously not heard of "The Three Assured Ps" that entrench the Man in Power: Pay, Pension and Pickings. Often well augmented by Pilfering by the greedy and corrupt native. Add Pillaging and extortion and it's assurance of a marvellously elastic – or should I say *Pliable*? – income!

  And how could I omit the other Ps: the buying of 4-Penny witnesses to Perjure themselves. These indigenes actually *like* getting up in the stand and *lying*: it seems to appeal to their betting spirit! The native is generally a cautious man, even the trading community isn't given to speculation. But he exercises a surprising gambling streak by going into litigation, trying to load the dice by buying witnesses to win his case. They should be sworn in to Perjury, not to truth!
- But doesn't Pax Brittanica ensure that everyone gets

justice in its courts?

- Sadly Victor, er *Pax Britannica* is a double-edged sword. It has brought English education, but what has that done for the er *Indian*? It only equips him for a life of idle anticipation. Or, that last resort of scoundrels, they take to law. Sorry Albert, present company excepted of course.
- I should think so: I *enforce* Pax Britannica, not twist it to crooked ends! But because the litigious natives believe our courts will give them justice, they flood us with frivolous cases, which line the pockets of barristers. And I'm condemned to crack those cases in the sweltering heat of what passes for a muffasil "courthouse", hemmed in with stinking peasants, as most cases have to do with land or money. That's how the native is bound in perpetual debt, either to the money lender or the lawyer.
- I've heard that our judges have a very difficult time of it if they have little or no knowledge of customary law, and because documentary proof is rare and written leases almost non-existent?
- Yes Victor, and because I don't know the local language, I have to rely on interpreters and pleaders between myself and litigants, giving these native court officers plenty of scope for corruption and dishonesty.
- Well, I suppose the legal side of Pax Brittanica brings some money into native pockets, no matter how dubiously obtained.
- What I find so dismaying is that er *"English educated"*

sons of farmers and tradesmen have learned only to despise their inherited callings. They don't deign to dirty their hands with their fathers' soil or coin. Their er *education* makes them supercilious and unfit for anything other than spending their time in hopeful indolence, waiting for that coveted Government Position. Such folly when the numbers are against them: look at the limited posts available as against the number of applicants!

~ At last we agree on one thing William: our education makes the native a misfit. To his detriment, he learns to ape all the outward signs of the sahib; wears trousers and shoes and, oh yes, what a glib tongue! And he takes drinking to be a sign of sophistication, so overdoes it, making him risible, losing the little native dignity he possesses.

11

- Oh dear Devaki, what a long face. Yes, I know, he's gone, but what did you expect? I kept telling you he would. So much for your luv-ve luv-ve ....
- Don't tease me now Annan. And don't mock love; love marriage is known in our tradition, 'kalavu'. Like Valli and Murugan. Don't look so surprised; yes I did pay some attention to my lessons.

Please, just listen to me, Annan. You're the only one I can talk to about what I'm feeling. Some time ago I tried to tell Amma and Appa that I felt an emptiness, a consuming yearning. But they interpret that as the most natural feeling of a human's need to merge with God.

And now I find it has absolutely nothing to do with

God and everything to do with a *man*, an outcaste at that, who has rendered me "totally polluted" according to our shastras. But I feel cleansed, not soiled. Union with him is the ablution that has washed away all those previously sordid degrading sexual encounters.

- You are polluted and will pollute the temple. Isn't that terrifying? And imagine what the Priest would do!
- Yes, he'd want to purify me with Gangajal and re-purifying rituals, but none of those could make me feel as untainted as I already feel, anointed as I have been by him.

At my 'prayojanam', I was told I was free to choose my lovers. Isn't that part of my profession?

- In theory yes. But you've never tried to put it into practice; you'd find it isn't that simple. And now you want to exercise your right by choosing a vellakāran, beyond our caste pale?
- What hypocrisy! So, even if my patron is of a low caste, my having sex with him doesn't contaminate the temple? But I *do* pollute if I've had a vellakāran? And isn't it ironic that our caste system is based on varna, wherein the darkest are considered so low that they are excluded from the four castes. But a foreigner, even though he is fairer than the fairest Brahmin, is considered even lower than the pariah! And what are we? I don't see that our community has much status...
- We are like a caste of our own because we take in any girls given to the temple no matter what caste, because they are purified by the dedication ritual.

We try to marry our own kind and are governed by our own rules. But sleeping with a vellakāran, that is going too far.

- And I, I don't even know what caste I was born to. Lakshmi used to taunt me about my colour. Once she called me a bastard who never knew her parents, not even my own mother … Is it true, Annan? I never wanted to ask Amma or Appa, for fear of hurting them. And it's the first time I'm even telling you. I love all of you so much that I could never think that you all weren't my real family.
- We are, we are … oh my poor sweet Devaki, we loved you from the first. Lakshmi was just petty and jealous, particularly because she wasn't as fair as you.
But I will tell you about your background ... well, I have to show you something first.

###

- You back here again, Albert?
- Unfortunately yes, Victor. This place is the centre for all the work in its surrounding areas, and my Joint is doing everything he can to see me out of the way. He feels that will draw Laetitia's attention away from me, as if he has the slightest chance!
Thank goodness this is a large enough town to have this TB. Considerably more civilized than some remote outpost where one would have to camp. Though one has to ride out quite far for game of any kind.

You up for shooting today?

- Any deer in these parts? A haunch of venison would make a nice change from the tough old chicken we've been eating.
- No deer, though we could easily get partridge or green pigeon if you're up to riding some distance.
- No more fowl of any kind please.
- Well, there's wild pig if we ride out later in the evening, about ten or fifteen miles from here. But we shouldn't bag too much otherwise the Sunday roast will turn up for the rest of the week as Irish stew, Lancashire hotpot, cottage pie, rissoles ... And when it's finally gone too high in this heat, then the servants take the remains. But the native cooks are ingenious, I'll give you that, the way they can turn out pretty decent meals with such limited and primitive resources.
- Yes, I'm amazed that they produce perfect puff-pastry with an "oven" that is nothing but a tin box, placed on a wood fire. I don't know how they can judge the temperature ....
- Oh, haven't you seen their "temperature control"? They put a piece of paper in it and see how long it takes to turn the shade of brown for what needs to be baked: different shades for a cake, steak and kidney pudding, or curry puffs. If the paper goes up in flames, the oven is too hot!

Not that Albert found Po-face particularly good company. The blasted chap was a teetotaller! And his delicate stomach was a constant boring topic of conversation at table. But he did read a lot so that gave them some common ground. And at least he was someone to talk to – servants didn't count of course – and ride out with.

###

- What's the matter Devaki? It's like the mood you always get into when it's that time of moon, only I know it isn't that ... Oh my god ... Are you …?

Clever Kumara; doesn't miss a trick, spots hormonal changes in a woman.

- I just can't believe you can be so stupid! You know how to take precautions. Why why, when you have been so careful all this time not to conceive?
- Yes, I never wanted children before, because what future could I give them? For a boy, only a musician; devadasi for a girl. What if he turned out to have no musical talent – like you – or she had no talent for dancing, as it was with Lakshmi? If he hated the arts, if he were born tone deaf with no aptitude for music and longed instead to sail away in a ship, or have a shop, or plough a plot of land?
- You've been most careful with your patron; well, he made it quite clear that he wouldn't maintain any child of yours.
- Huh, as if I'd want *his* child in any case …

~ And now this mleccha's child?

~ But this, I *want* my dorai's child.

~ Pah, "dorai, dorai" – you don't even know his *name*!

~ So when he came here the second time, I didn't do anything to prevent conception. But I'm not even completely sure I am carrying. Don't you see, he will *have* to keep me if I have his child!

~ So he doesn't know you're carrying his child?

~ I told you I'm not sure, but I'm going to tell him I *am* pregnant. The child will be a part of him and I'm sure it will bind him to me. I am willing to give up everything, if I can have this child and go away with him. I know I can't live in his house if he marries some doraisani. But at least till then … or even if he pays me some money for me to live somewhere with this child and he just sees us sometimes.

I'll tell him I can be his servant, I will do any work. I can be an ayah when he has children with a doraisani. But he must take me away with him.

~ I'm going to get that plant to abort it and you have to take it immediately. You are definitely not even three months' gone.

~ No, I'm not going to get rid of the love I'm carrying.

~ You come to Appa right now. He will tell you what you have to do. It'll just finish Amma off if she comes to know. She's been so ill recently.

~ Oh god no, please don't tell Amma. She's already in so much pain. But Appa can say nothing to change my mind.

She rose to leave.

- No wait. You have to listen to what Appa has to say about all this. If you don't agree to at least talk to him, then I will tell Amma. So you choose.
- Why do we have to tell him? Why don't you just help me run away with my dorai, fine brother you are! Yes yes, I know I will only be a concubine, his keep, but that's no different from what I already am here!
- Don't forget, by 'puravalar' keeping you he gains in status. He is seen as a man who can afford a devadasi. You also gain status: you are kept by a rich man. What can this vellakāran give you? You will have to live in an outhouse with the other servants. But worse than a servant, you'll be kept secreted away from his family and society, a shame he keeps hidden. You won't be able to eat with him, or say anything to him except through that swine Ja-ahn. You'll have to sneak into the house when it's dark and no one else can see you. Is that what you want, even worse than a street woman, who at least does what she does openly? Oh Devaki, how can I save you from hurt and pain? And how can I live without you if you leave? He will surely cast you away when you become an inconvenience. Who will take care of you then?
- Don't cry, my dear dear Annan. If I go, be happy for me.
- Happy ... what is happiness? Not my desire which is shameful, love that is not allowed to be expressed. Concealment ... but I have learned to live with all

that. Ever since you came to know what I really am, I can tell you what I go through. You don't know how much that means to me, to be able to talk to you about what I feel, knowing you will not judge or rebuke. It makes me feel you are the half of me that I am not allowed to look for in a man. It's only my love for you that makes me feel somewhat … complete.

- Oh Annan Annan, perhaps in another 'janam': may be in our next lives we will truly be together.

  Oh no, here's Appa. I hope he hasn't seen me. I really don't want to talk to him now.
- Appa, only you can talk some sense into this stupid girl.
- Yes, I was looking for you, rājāthi ....
- See Devaki, he knows. I told you it would become common knowledge.
- Fortunately, it's not quite that yet, but we have to do something about it before it is.
- Appa, luv-ve, luv-ve with this vellakaran, that is all she can talk about. She thinks he's different from other men.

True, Devaki interpreted the manifestations of Albert's cultural differences – his sexual techniques – as "love". She had no prior experience of foreplay and titillation, and mistook his lewdness for admiration. But it was also true that Albert had often been unable to suppress spontaneous pleasure when he sank with sated exhaustion, after experiencing her exceptional sexual prowess. Since reflective equivocations of language were by-passed, Devaki could not be wholly blamed for imbuing his immediate satisfaction with deeper feeling.

- I've warned her that luv-ve is certain ruination.
- Yes, Appa, love. All this yearning I have felt since my initiation, suddenly I knew what that emptiness was … what my heart had asked a hundred times, I have now found words to express.

  "Love", I hear this word in every padam, but how could I only be beckoning a god who will never come? It has nothing to do with god at all. It is with *him*, my dorai, that I finally realised what union means and it became conceivable that that Shaivite symbol, seen so prosaically everywhere, could stand for bliss.

  And I now make the surrender willingly, with all of my body. And can't you see it isn't just my body, it's with *all* of my being. Only now do I see the wholeness, the words of the songs that my body has translated; that craving, expansion that leaves not just a vast emptiness here, but fills the aching void I've always felt.

  Completion, not depletion, his expanding in me, expansion which unites me with him.
- And have you thought about the future with this great love of yours, rājāthi?
- Oh oh, look what a cloud crosses thy face. Well? Why don't you tell Appa what you were telling me?
- Appa, can't I go away with him? Live with him?
- And what about your dance?

- Oh, another cloud ....
- You are here to dance, while your body is still capable of it, you have to dance. And yes, fulfil all the other duties of your role in this temple, in this given life. Look at it as transcendent bounty.

  What can your vellakāran do for you? You serve *him*, in lieu of an inspiring God? Do not mock heaven so! Your so-called love is attained by sacrilege ....
- An apostate apsara ....
- Be quiet, Kumara. Much of what I say about lust, love, devotion, applies to you too.

  Service to god must come from an innocent and pure hunger for Unity with the Divine, impossible as long as there is a maddening addiction to mere appetites.
- But he is the sun, the sun that will show me myself in the person of my shadow, in the absence of a mirror.
- Āhahā, what poetry …! Why don't you get him out of your system by writing a poem about separation, unrequited love, the object of desire being beyond your reach, too far above you ….
- Quiet, Kumara. But Devaki, you are not a separate entity tethered to the shadow by that earthly limitation called love. Your art embodies all of human potential and is aggrandised for a greater glory, not to be overcast by the cloud of human lust.
- Lust, *lust*?! Lust is what's shown by 'puravalar', the man who beds me while I have to feign obsequious worship. What nauseating dispensation, for one's soul to be obliterated by such men, instead of by God! My

role of deva-dasi – "blessed servant to god" – is now just carnality and profit. *That* is profanation, not my love for a vellakāran!

- Yes, unfortunately what you have to do with 'puravalar' has nothing to do with your relationship to God. But the alarming thing is that you now want to believe that your vellakāran is not like all men, but that *he* is the *God*. Such a surrogate idol leaves you with ....
- ... feet of clay? Oh sorry, wrong term, Appa. How could she dance then? So that makes the vellakāran an idol with feet of clay.
- Oh, be quiet Kumara. Yes Devaki, it's unfortunate that lascivious services and divine sacraments have now to co-exist in your role, which didn't originate like this. Develop detachment when you serve men. That is the only way you can unite such irreconcilable forces in yourself; be wrenched by them, and it is sure self-destruction.

###

William came back exhausted but exhilarated with his findings, not that the two other men showed much interest. Well, maybe his father would.

- I don't know how you tolerate scouring that scrub and rock for your "finds". I find any posting out of Madras a hardship, now that I have a special interest there!
- Well Albert, my area of special interest is obviously

very er *different* from yours.

Any developments for you, Victor?

- Looks like I may well be tied to scrub and rock as well, William, once I'm done in this area. Madras Presidency has such arid countryside. They'll probably base me in a muffasil next.

Victor dreaded the thought of being alone in a remote muffasil. He couldn't confide in William about the confusion that often overcame him, when even the Bible couldn't fortify him, couldn't keep out the erotic thoughts with native women that assailed him. He had always had such vigour, rarely fatigued by hard work. He couldn't understand this lassitude that now often overcame him. Even the soporific sway of the punka seemed to pinion him to its small square of influence. Or was this the Empire striking back: leaching Saxon energy, replacing it with the native's lethargy.

- Oh, but muffasils can be interesting when there's a minor raja or nawab about.

  I was invited by one to a concert of Indian music, though that wasn't amusing. Blasted thing threatened to go on for as long as a cricket match! That endless droning; it was all I could do not to fall asleep! I made my getaway with the excuse that I had an early start the next day.

- I'm so lucky to have Muthu with me on my expeditions. He's also actually er *interested* in what I find.

- Is he educated?

- No Victor, that's the thing. So much er *potential.* Well, my mother did teach him the 3 R-s; she insisted all our servants went through it! And she encouraged them to share their local habits and stories and folklore with us.
  Muthu was our cook's son, so he worked himself up from scullion to cook's mate and now he's a very good bearer, though he's more than that really. He's thrilled that I take him on my travels. But it's a pity Muthu hasn't had time to pursue his basic English. I must see how he can take it up again.

###

At dinner, Victor was "suitably attired", drawing such approval as Albert was capable of expressing:

- Well well well, Victor, here you are, dressed even better than the chicken!
- Oh no, not Sudden Death served up yet again. When I see my dinner being chased around squawking, before it comes to the table, it puts me off. Oh, I know that it has to be killed if we are to eat chicken; it's just that I don't care to see the process before it's served up.
- Well Victor, we do the same with game, don't we? So I don't see what all the fuss is about with chickens.
- No Albert, we don't go around chasing deer, partridge or duck brandishing a cleaver and yelling. *That's* the difference. And so often they botch it so that

the chicken is running around with its head cut off. Awful!

- Turn vegetarian Victor, you'll fit right in with the natives. In any case you are such an ascetic; doesn't look as if you *ever* enjoy your food.
- Oh I love these! I asked the cook to get some from the bazaar. They're called poppadams here but I still remember when we first landed in Bombay and I couldn't eat any of the native food. What I could have were these Popper Cakes because they weren't spicy. Yes, that's what they're called in Bombay, because they puff up like little balloons when fried. And I loved popping them! They're still one of my favourite foods.
- Oh Victor, I spoke too soon, here's something you actually *savour*! You're making me eat my words, not my favourite dish I can tell you: words don't do much by way of nourishment or filling the belly. And now, if you'll excuse me, I'm off to satisfy other appetites!

12

– Appa said I must make you take that medicine but I couldn't find that root where it usually grows. I'll see if there's any left in Amma's medicine box. God only knows how many times she's had to take it.

– But if I do abort, then why do I even have to think of leaving here? No one needs to know that I've been pregnant.

– You think Guruggal doesn't know you've been seeing your vellakarān? He's just waiting .... I don't know why or for what, but I'm sure he knows.

– How, how? How could he possibly know, when even Amma doesn't?

– Amma's been too ill to notice much. First get rid of it, then we'll wait and see if Amma or Guruggal say anything. If they do and you have to leave, then we'll have to see what we can do.

– Couldn't we run away together, somewhere far, where no one will recognise us? We can say we are husband and wife. It would be convenient for both of us.

– What would we live on?

– Can't we go to a city where we could find jobs, as servants or something?

– You would end up in the brothels of Madras, and your child would soon follow, selling its body. Oh, how the pimps would love a fair child, girl or boy. They could demand an enormous amount of money for a fair virgin, either sex.

And don't think a boy would be spared: I've told you that some men go to brothels to have boys, but you don't believe me. Oh, with his white moon buttocks he would be in great demand! And for those men that only want their cocks sucked off, the pimps extract the boy's teeth and have him chew sugarcane so that his gums become hard and can give maximum pleasure.

I know you don't like hearing about that side of my life, but I've been around and heard about such things from men and boys who've had to do such things.

I wouldn't be fit for anything except selling my body. To earn any money, we'd both end up doing that.

Yes, Kumara was one of those males who lived off the indulgence of women. His roguish charm and well-placed flattery ensured that. He was occasionally pressed into service as gopher and general factotum, but was never trained to earn a living.

> [Promila: It's amazing how many men in India still enjoy this privilege, living off the labour of mothers, sisters, daughters.
> Sagarika: Even grandmothers! My parents' maid is a grandmother. She's not really that old; that generation got married very young. But she's the only one that works in her family: her husband's a drunk, so can't hold down a job; her son is disabled so demands that his wife has to stay home to look after him, so she doesn't get any time to do the housework. Her grandchildren go to college, but they don't even help at home when they come back. So this grandmother is not only the sole bread-winner, she has to do the cooking and housework in her own home, even after a full day's work at my mother's!
> Fiona: Typical! Indian children are so spoiled. No wonder so few want to leave home, even after they get jobs.
> SD: Well, that is partly because accommodation is so expensive. Even a white-collar worker can afford to get his/her own flat only if he/she gets a loan.
> Akhil: And there's always the convenience of having in situ baby sitters.
> Bhaumi: Yes, there are advantages of a joint family. In fact, some in the west are adopting it, though

in a modified form that will give independence to the young couple as well as security to the older generation.]

###

Albert was in the area on a hasty trip and couldn't resist sending for Devaki again. After all, it would be the last time; he was hurrying back to discuss wedding plans with Laetitia, as she had, "of course!", accepted him.

Devaki rushed to Kumara, full of excitement.

- He's come again, thank god! Now I can tell him I'm carrying his child. I'm sure he'll take me or make arrangements for me to follow him later.
- But you're not even sure you're pregnant, so you're going to lie?
- So what? As long as he believes it and wants to keep me. Then, if I find I'm not pregnant, I'll go to the 'valluvan' and get some herb to ensure that I conceive. So what if the baby is born later rather than sooner. My dorai's not going to calculate.

Kumara was familiar with her stubbornness. In the face of it, he could only try to help her in her insane plan. But he first had to tell her about her parentage; he'd put it off longer than he intended, but there just hadn't been the right time. Maybe, just maybe, the vellakāran would be more likely to accept Devaki and her child – in some unofficial capacity, of course – if he knew that Devaki had an English father. Did he want to abandon his child the way that man had?

Kumara had noticed the bundle that came with the infant Devaki, but his natural curiosity was sidelined by his preoccupation with the baby. Years later, when he was raiding his mother's wardrobe to satisfy his cross-dressing urges, he saw the bundle placed in the highest shelf, behind other innocuous stacks of clothes. Certainly not a place where Devaki would look for anything.

Kumara had overheard the conversation between his mother and Kamala but knew better than to reveal that fact to his parents. He had sensed that they were cagey about Devaki's antecedents and he realised that they were trying to shield her from the hurt of being rejected by her biological parents.

- I have something to give you. I found it in the bundle of clothes Amma brought with you as a baby.

The photograph had faded, but it was still apparent that the only dark face was that of a young woman, obviously the ayah, carrying an infant. Oddly, the background – the house and garden – would still be recognisable to one who knew the property.

- Who are these people?
- That's your mother. She was an ayah in that Madras household, and that boy sitting on the horse took her sexually. He's your father.

  I've always known you had other parents. When we went to have Lakshmi's foot treated, I overheard your birth-mother tell Amma that the son of the house, the baba-dorai, was your father. But I just knew I wasn't supposed to mention your "other parents". And I was so taken with you that all of my being wanted you to be part of our family, so I pushed aside all thoughts of your different parentage.

Did you never suspect?

- Well, of course I can see I'm fairer, but I felt I was different in some way because Lakshmi made me feel unwanted. But after she left, I didn't give it much thought, till my dorai made me feel that he liked my skin.

Clutching the photograph, Devaki sobbed.

- Show this to your great love. It might just prompt his conscience to support you and his child.
- Oh Annan, if I have white blood, I want him to know. Do you think he'll keep me if I could prove it to him … that I am not just a pariah servant like his Ja-ahn? How I long to hold a lovely fat baby, as creamy as the moon, maybe with blue eyes like his looking into mine, with his smile … I'll remember my dorai forever if I could hold part of him like that. I know my heart will never be empty of him; let my arms, too, have their share.
- Oh god, poetry at this stage? You need action, not words!
- I could be his servant. After all, I now know my own mother was that.

> Huh, you think his doraisani will employ you? No one will, if you turn up with a 'kāpi'-coloured baby on your hip! It will be a warning to everyone, to keep their husbands and sons away from you.
> And it will be even worse if you tried to get employment in an Indian household. You know what they call girls like you.

She soon shook herself free of the comforting Kumara and, taking the photograph, composed herself to go on her assignation.

###

It was a hurried trip for Albert who had been rushed to the area to deal with a very pressing case and had summoned the litigant after breakfast the next morning. Albert had arrived earlier in the afternoon than he expected, so sent John off immediately, anticipating several hours of a leisurely display of all the girl's skills, interspersed with sufficient bouts of recovery for him.

However, it was not the ideal last encounter with Devaki that Albert had hoped for. As soon as she entered the room, he was irritated to be given a photograph, with much gesticulation on her part, pointing out two figures and miming that those were her parents. Albert had not the time, inclination or interest to pay it any heed. What a waste of time! He thrust the photograph into a book, and eagerly shucked off his clothes. He'd just disrobed her and was in the first throes of passion when John discreetly interrupted with a message that Albert was to return to Madras *forthwith*. Therefore John, with ubiquitous efficiency, had taken the liberty of sending for the litigant immediately. If dorai could see him at once, they could leave as soon as the interview was over, and they could reach Madras late in the night, with the urgent information that was required.

Albert hastily dressed for his appointment, cursing the premature termination of his desire. Though Devaki was surprised at the sudden interruption of their session, she didn't dress. It was still early afternoon: it was obvious dorai was just going to deal with some emergency and would soon be back. Till John, noticing that she hadn't emerged from the room, was at his sneering best when he barged in and threw money on the table.

- Get dressed and clear off.
- But isn't dorai coming back? I can wait.
- Not here you can't. Wait in your temple, all you want. You won't be coming here again. My dorai is getting married soon. Very nice doraisani in Madras ... going to be a very grand wedding!

  Āhahā, you thought you were something special or what? Huh, he's had plenty like you.
- But I might be carrying his child ....
- So, get rid of it, keep it ... what's it to him? He probably has a few running around the countryside.

###

- Devaki, the Priest wants to see you. Go now.
- Oh god, Appa why? Does he know? What did he say to you? Ayyō, where's Kumara?
- He sent word that he wants to see you – *alone*, so in any case Kumara couldn't have gone with you. The Priest has sent him to town, to get Amma medicines.

Devaki naturally feared the worst, assuming the Priest had heard what she'd been doing. Ironic timing; it was all over in any case, as she wouldn't see her vellakāran again. At least she could tell the Priest that, and promise to reform and do whatever was necessary to make her acceptable again.

- I haven't seen you for some days, Devaki?
- You haven't been well and I didn't want to disturb you. But, don't worry, Guruggal, I've been carrying on my duties as usual. And I have been seeing to Amma. She's very sick.
- Yes, I heard. I've sent Kumara to town; maybe he can bring the doctor to come and see her tomorrow. Or Kumara will return tomorrow afternoon with the medicines. And I have sent for Shankara to come and see me, after you go home after the last dance and puja.
- Please, please pray for Amma.
- Oh my dear girl, do you think prayers work? If they did, wouldn't I have saved myself? All the mantras, rituals, pujas … yes, I wonder why I did them all when I was always sceptical.

Huhn, smoke from sacrificial fires sending up the prayers of craven supplicants to heaven, leaving the ash of unfulfilled wishes and desires, vibhuthi to apply to the forehead, like rubbing salt into wounds. Listen, I know I don't have time left. No no … I don't need any sympathy or sops about how I'm sure to recover... I just want to talk about my ... life ... not looking for absolution or anything like that ....

Devaki was worried. He was perspiring and restless; was he delirious? But she didn't dare interrupt and soon found he was coherent, even cogent.

- I've often told you about the life-force, that life-force that reverberates in everything and should pervade your dance. Well, I celebrated it in sensual ravening. And since God sees everything, I've given that voyeur an eyeful!

It was as if he were addressing not only her, but the heavens: a defiant declaration, his parting shot, interspersed with spasms of coughing and fits of mocking laughter.

- Predestination and free will: are they ever in conflict, or can they co-exist? I have challenged Fate with the most flagrant displays of willpower.

  My options were yogi or bhogi, ascetic or hedonist. Yes, those rhyming Hindu pairs – well, after all our aim is to go beyond dualities. My favourite twins were ever with me: Kama and Yama; Eros and Thanatos, the Greeks call them. Kama's bow is strung with bees and his shafts, flower-bedecked though they are, are still arrows.

Aye, there's the barb.

I experienced the Janus-faced Kama and Yama together. Embracing Kama, I found myself face to face with Yama instead! But of late, Yama's been getting to my brain, unfortunately not in the delightful way Kama used to.

Therein lies the greatest sensuality: imagination-fuelled sex! Thank god for my fervid imagination which endowed with lust almost everything I saw.

The Midas touch, what's the sexual equivalent? I was satisfied if those I touched were turned to lust. Better than turning them to dust! Ha ha ha ... I allowed Kama to draw and draw on my – well, let's call it "account" – but now Yama has foreclosed on me. Oh Yama, in all my enjoyment of Kama I've experienced you simultaneously. I have given my life-force to Kama, but Yama, I glimpsed you at that supreme moment of life itself, for it is also a kind of dying ....

"The little death", the French call it.

So I've been practising death all my life! Existential caprice.

To be intensely aware of time encapsulates it. To feel the vitality of an orgasm is temporary immunity from time, raises your consciousness of the eternal.

I lived inconsequentially perhaps, but *intensely* so.
Now Yama'll yank on his noose: unfortunately it's not around as painless a part of my anatomy as my neck! But no matter. Kama's chariot has given me a rollicking good ride. And I daresay when Yama bears me away, his buffalo's bristles will chafe away at what's left of my tender diseased parts – *deceased* parts, ha ha! If all the sexual stimulation poor Yama gets is his buffalo ride, no wonder he's envious, bounty hunting every profligate like me.
Oh what the hell, the maya's been wonderful. I've skipped out for some intermissions, but on the whole I've been glued to my seat, you know with what ….
But not even the oozing and the itching and this pox-fermented brain can bring me to dharmic heel.
I've robbed them of that sweet revenge.

But his belief that he had earned a kind of redemption in the thoroughness of his sins, now wavered.

(Sigh) Or have I? In my voracity I tried to obliterate the past. Recall the past and it perpetually returns in troubled repetitiousness. Acknowledge the past and it traps you into responsibility, for you are then held accountable for your actions.
I regarded the present tense as all, trying to deny that time future is ever with us. Instant gratification made me feel as if I was outracing the immediacy of an inevitable end.
But no, unfortunately it doesn't all end now.

> (Sigh). There's the afterlife to come. Just when you think you've swept all the karmic dust-balls under the carpet, you move on to the next room and find you still need the old broom.
>
> Anyway, I've achieved my definition of immortality: the full enjoyment of my allotted life-span. As the prayer goes, "May I fall from the tree only when my time is ripe. May I not be plucked untimely thereof".
>
> I don't seek that other kind of immortality, to live forever. That's boring, and it corrupts. Look at our gods: malicious meddling in human lives, petty jealousy of rishis whom they see as rivals ....
>
> Yes, I know I impress you all with learning. But what has all my knowledge come to, eh? The Vedas, shastras, the privilege of my birth, nothing has availed in the curbing of my appetites, my sex-propelled existence to rocket me, not into oblivion, but to the next circle.

Tiers in swarga and naraka, Dante's Circles, though his Purgatory pales when compared to descriptions of Dharmaraja's time in Hell.

> "In my Father's house are many mansions". But no room booked for me there. I hope I'll be reborn as a fly, so that I can continue to eat the prasad of the gods. But I can also sit on shit, or dine with kings, at will, ha ha ha. And, every so often, I'll come here and settle on the nipple of this glorious Devi and watch some beauty dance.

He was exhausted after his long confession, but

managed the most important thing he had summoned her to hear:

- Devaki ... I know, I *know* about you. Like me, you have challenged god, karma ... shown courage, because you are incapable of acting in any other way ... you struck out, *acted*. Acedia: being apathetic, that's the greatest sin.
  You are the inheritor of my life-force that disdains convention ... defies extinction ... dauntless to the grave.
  Now *go* ....

But the Priest's unexpected endorsement had come too late.

###

William returned to the TB that evening, full of excitement after one of his long archaeological forays.

- I finally located those er *megalithic* burial sites I was keen to find. They have given me so much to work on! You on your own, Victor? Oh, Albert's left has he? Pity, I wanted to borrow a book from him.
- He rushed off after some sudden summons that came in the middle of his "liaison". Ooh, he wasn't pleased about that interruption! But he managed a few words with me. Was full of his imminent wedding.
  Which book are you looking for? He's left three behind, I'm reading the Dickens. This photograph

was in it.

You're going to see him in Madras aren't you? You can return the books to him … and the photograph, if he wants it.

- This photograph …?!
- When I asked him, he was in such a flurry to leave, that he just mumbled something about that girl having shown it to him, claiming her parents were in it.
- *What*? But these were my neighbours in Madras: that's little Elaine and Anthony with their parents, the Smythes! So that er *ayah* was her mother?

Good heavens, do you know what this means? Isn't it obvious? The girl apparently has white blood in her, we all remarked on her unusual colour.

Oh-*ho*, that sly dog "Mr Smythe"! I knew that he seemed too holier than thou!! Come on Victor, you can't be that naïve.

Reginald Smythe must be her er *father*!

- I'm not sure what ...
- What *exactly* did Albert tell you about the photograph?
- Nothing other than what I've already told you. He had to leave in the most frightful hurry so he was most dismissive, not in the least interested in her antecedents!
- Don't you see, Victor? If Mr Smythe is her father but hasn't even been aware of her er *existence*, he might want to do something for her. Hmm, probably on the quiet, for if they are anything like they used to be,

they certainly wouldn't acknowledge her publicly.

I heard he's retiring soon and that Mrs Smythe's already left for England. I'll have to track down Old Smithee before he leaves. He might just do the right thing by this girl.

- Leave well enough alone, William, is what I say.

William didn't remonstrate with him as he was too excited by his discovery. But there was something vaguely disturbing about the photograph, something that unsettled him, though he couldn't point to any one feature, or even an expression that could lay a genetic smear; no snail trail from the stiff cardboard in his hand to the sprightly lovely girl he'd seen.

- I've just got to speak to her and find out exactly what she knows.

  Muthu, Muthu ... I'll give you a letter to take to that girl in the temple. Yes, I'm quite sure she *can* read Tamil.

  Just make sure you go to the temple first thing tomorrow morning, give her this letter – and *bring her here.*

  I just can't wait to see her reaction when I tell her I knew her parents! And what her father might be able to do for her.

###

That evening in the temple Devaki chose to dance

Krishna nee bégané bārō, begging Krishna to come quickly, in her desperate attempt to displace the white god with the blue. That most evocative padam, was about the longing of the supplicant to be united with the loved one: surely Krishna would have accepted her carnal yearnings, her deep and intense love for a man, as a parallel offering to Himself?

Her beloved Amma had always said her dancing lacked something. She would have been proud to see that Devaki had finally captured the dance's essence, though ironically, she had been able to do so only after experiencing a forbidden love. Devaki's last pleading dance gesture was for God to come, with all the yearning of bhakti and sringara in her pose, hands, face, with the realisation that her first love had to be God, as she finally accepted that the other temporal love was irrevocably lost.

The Priest had retired soon after the puja, to relieve his pain with goodness knows what opiate, so it wasn't difficult for Devaki to sneak into the room in which the 'kattari' was kept and smuggle it home.

###

Mangala called out hoarsely for some water but Devaki did not rush to her dutifully.

- Devaki, Devaki ...?? What's the time? Has she gone to pick flowers?

Mangala even called out to Shankara, she who had

never asked him to do anything for her.

- Yéngō yéngō ... please get me some water ....

Where was he? She thought she'd heard a door slamming, but she couldn't be sure when ... or if she'd just dreamed it, that palliative had made her so groggy. She tossed about trying to take her weight off the pain. At least one of them should be home ...?

- Devaki De-va-kee! Water water ... Kumara Kumara ...?

A blur of him saying he was going away ... with one of his dance troupes?

- Water water ... if a person drinks water just before dying, that's a blessing ... I will be borne across .... Just give me a drink of water ... whoever administers that water will be doubly blessed, don't they know that ?... Who will that be ...?

###

Devaki laid the 'kattari' on the bridal bed.

- I married you, and now at last I can find use for you. Husband, my life became yours, so now take it. What better sacrifice can a servant perform for her master, a wife for her husband, than offer her life to him – and perhaps more than just *one* life ...?

  Why only a lime thrust on your point, oh surrogate god – don't you deserve more than such sourness? Why not an actual yoni, mine?

I remember so clearly when I wed you, I wished I had brought the lovely red brocade piece to decorate you, the one I used to wrap around my beloved wooden doll. You were so dull, I wondered why I had dressed up so much for you, with more jewellery than I had ever worn, in the gorgeous sari heavy with gold, surrounded by music, joyousness ....

Lying next to you was easy; I wished that was the end of my "marriage". I only realised when I was sent to my patron, what the real dagger thrust was, with blood, pain ... soreness for days after. And then the thickened skin.

But those lesions soon became indifferent to all the matings that followed, by which time the welts in my heart let me feign delight, ecstasy, passion, all that Amma taught me.

Not until I met my dorai did I finally discover all those "higher feelings" which I never believed possible, never thought could exist.

And now it's all over. So pierce me, on this bed, the very bed on which you "consummated" my marriage to God. And maybe you can also take, in my river of blood, the mleccha foetus I think I am carrying.

###

No Puccini to commemorate the sacrifice. Sacrifice, an appropriately loaded word for a devadasi. Madame Butterfly, almost the same age, almost contemporaneous with Devaki, though worlds apart … Butterfly would have understood. Sepukku: Butterfly's sword was given to her by her father, with the directive to use it when she could no longer live in honour, thereby enabling her to die with honour. Devaki's weapon was also given to honour her, as God's bride no less, but never with an injunction to use it, least of all to turn it on herself.

But why shouldn't it finally claim her: for she was Devaki, God's own.

###

Maya Goray is the pen name of a multifaceted author. On graduating from Delhi University with a BA in English Honours, she has been writing for several newspapers and journals, focusing on the arts. An avid reader and traveller, she is currently writing a children's play. *Devadasi* was largely inspired by her interest in Raj history. Having learned Odissi dance, her interest extends to Bharathnatyam. Her other interests are bird-watching and the opera. Maya is married, with two children and makes her home in India.